The Mysteries of Heron Dyke

A Novel of Incident.

Volume 3

GW01066320

T. W. Speight

Alpha Editions

This edition published in 2024

ISBN : 9789361470448

Design and Setting By
Alpha Editions
www.alphaedis.com
Email - info@alphaedis.com

As per information held with us this book is in Public Domain.
This book is a reproduction of an important historical work. Alpha Editions uses the
best technology to reproduce historical work in the same manner it was first
published to preserve its original nature. Any marks or number seen are left
intentionally to preserve its true form.

Contents

CHAPTER I.

WHO DID IT?

Never as long as Ella Winter lives will she forget the picture that imprinted itself on her brain, as instantaneously as though it had been photographed there, at the moment when, startled by Aaron Stone's cry, she stepped out of the window of the sitting-room. On the borders of the lawn, at the foot of a large holly-bush, the leaves of which glistened brightly in the morning sun, knelt Aaron, his rugged features working convulsively, his trembling arms twined round the unconscious form of him who lay there in all the moveless majesty of death. One glance at the white set face, and Ella knew that the wanderer, whose absence had caused so much speculation, had come back at last, but that whatever secrets he might have in his keeping would remain secrets still, and would never be whispered in mortal ear. The pulses of her life stood still as she gazed in her shock of bewilderment.

The old man's voice broke the spell: he saw her standing there.

"Oh, ma'am, my dear young mistress, it is my boy! My boy come back to me--dead. There has been murder done here!"

A shudder ran through Ella. Murder! Was it true?--or was old Aaron demented?

She rushed indoors to the sitting-room, ringing its bells as they had never been rung before; and then she sank into a chair. Never had Ella Winter been so near fainting.

The servants came running in, and she strove to collect her thoughts. Some one ran to the huge bell that rang in the stable-yard, and sounded a peal upon it. It brought forth the coachman, Barnet. John Tilney came up with one of his men.

Barnet satisfied himself that Hubert Stone was really dead, also that he had in all probability been murdered; he then sped back to his stable-yard, and saddled a horse to ride forth in search of a doctor. "Fetch the nearest doctor you can find," had been Miss Winter's gasping order to him, and he hastened to obey it. By Barnet's orders the groom rode forth on another horse to summon the chief-constable from his office at Nullington.

The frightened maids had gathered round Miss Winter, when Dorothy Stone appeared in the doorway, tying her cap-strings with trembling fingers. The bells and the commotion had startled her, but she did not know what had happened. At sight of the patient, furrowed face and the dim blue eyes, just now full of anxious wonder, a great pity took the heart of Miss Winter, and the tears filled her own eyes as she went up to the old woman and led her away. No need for her to know the terrible news just yet.

Mrs. Toynbee next appeared upon the scene; she had waited to dress. Her first act was to order the white-faced servants away to their duties; her second to speak with John Tilney. It was by her directions that he and his two men--for the other man had come up now--carried the ill-fated young fellow into a room on the ground-floor. Then, with much tact and gentleness, Mrs. Toynbee succeeded in persuading Aaron, who seemed half-stupefied with grief and horror, to allow himself to be got into his own apartments by Tilney. Nothing more could be done till the arrival of the doctor and the police.

Dr. Spreckley and Mr. Chief-Constable Wade reached Heron Dyke together, driving over in a gig from the Rose and Crown. The first thing they did was to look at the dead. That Hubert Stone had been murdered a very slight examination sufficed to prove. He had been stabbed through the heart with a stiletto or some other sharp instrument. The disordered state of his attire, as well as the condition of the trimly-kept gravel walk, showed that he had not met his fate without a struggle; some desperate encounter must have taken place.

But what had brought him there? Why had he come back to Heron Dyke in the night-time?--or perhaps it might have been at the first glimmer of dawn. These were the questions that ran around. Miss Winter's thoughts, which she kept to herself, ran in somewhat a different groove. Might he not have come back by train the previous day, she asked herself, and have intended to call on her in the evening, and been afraid or ashamed to do so, and so have lingered about the grounds until it was too late? Too late also, perhaps, to gain admittance to his old rooms at the lodge? and so he had probably paced about during the night hours, and had disturbed the thief or thieves in the act of rifling the bureau Miss Winter's mind lost itself in troubled conjectures.

Examination showed that a hole had been cut with a diamond in the window of the room where the jewels lay, the window opened, and the shutters forced from their hinges. The bureau must then have been opened by means of a chisel, or other blunt instrument, and the jewels stolen from their receptacle. Most probably it was at the moment the burglar was leaving the room with his booty that he was encountered by Hubert Stone; perhaps seized by him. How the probably unequal struggle had ended was but too terribly manifest. Apparently nothing in Hubert's pockets had been touched. His watch, chain, and leather purse were all there, but no letters or papers of any kind from which a clue might be obtained as to his recent movements, or to the place from whence he had come.

"His watch has stopped at twenty minutes past two," observed Dr. Spreckley, who was making this examination with Mr. Inspector Wade. "And that may have been the time of the fatal occurrence, poor fellow. What's in here, I wonder?"

The Doctor was opening the gold locket attached to the watch-chain, as he made the last remark. And it was as well, perhaps, all things considered, that the inspector did not hear it--that he had turned momentarily away. For inside the locket was a portrait of Miss Winter. Dr. Spreckley's eyes opened, in more ways than one.

"Presuming rascal!" he involuntarily cried, apostrophising the unconscious dead. "My poor young man, you must have been more silly than I gave you credit for. I'll take possession of this, any way: no good to let the world see it," he decided, as he dexterously removed the likeness and slipped it into his waistcoat pocket.

"What's that?" asked the inspector, coming back.

"Only this," said Dr. Spreckley, exhibiting the empty locket.

That the person or persons who committed the robbery had also committed the murder, appeared perfectly conclusive to Inspector Wade; and so he informed Miss Winter, with whom he requested an interview. Of course she had herself drawn the same conclusion. He then asked Miss Winter whether she had the slightest suspicion with regard to the honesty of any of her servants. It was quite evident that the thieves must have had some acquaintance with the house, and knew the exact spot where to look for the jewels, and they had apparently made no attempt to obtain any other booty.

Miss Winter replied, in most decisive terms, that she had not the slightest reason to suspect the honesty of any person about her.

"But, indeed," she added, "it is impossible that any of the servants can be guilty. They were not even aware of the existence of the jewels, much less of the place where they were deposited. Those were facts known to no one save myself and Mrs. Toynbee."

The chief-constable, who had a pencil in his hand, passed it once or twice thoughtfully across his lips.

"Pardon me the remark, Miss Winter," he said, looking up, "but may I ask how it came to pass that you found no safer receptacle for this valuable amount of property than an old bureau in a sitting-room on the ground-floor--and which has a window opening to the ground? Any tyro of a burglar could force an entrance in ten minutes."

"But," she objected, "how was any burglar to know that such property was there?"

"It seems, madam, that one, at all events, did know it. It--pardon me--seems like throwing temptation in a thief's way."

"I again repeat that their being deposited there, and also that such jewels were in existence, was an entire secret between myself and Mrs. Toynbee," she replied. "Had it not been so, I should have removed them to a safer place. If you will listen a moment, Mr. Wade, I will tell you how it all came about, and how the jewels were found."

He listened as she related the facts: how she had caused this long-unopened old carved bureau to be brought downstairs to her morning-room, that she might search it for certain papers relating to the estate, which she fancied might be in existence. She failed to find the papers; but, to her intense surprise, she found, in a secret drawer, this large quantity of jewels. Mrs. Toynbee was present, and she had warned her that nothing must be said to the servants. Mrs. Toynbee fully agreed with her. After examining the jewels, they were replaced in their hiding-place, until she could see Mr. Daventry, and talk the affair over with him.

"It is impossible," concluded Miss Winter, looking at the inspector, "that the facts can have become known."

Mr. Wade, somewhat mystified, made no reply for a moment or two.

"But you cannot fail to see, madam," he urged, "that the fact of your having found the jewels must have leaked out somehow, as well as a knowledge of the place where they were placed. This burglary was no mere happy-go-lucky affair; it was evidently premeditated--carefully planned beforehand."

"It certainly does seem like it," admitted Ella. "But I assure you I cannot understand it. Mrs. Toynbee----"

"I think I had better see Mrs. Toynbee."

Mrs. Toynbee was called in, and came, full of nervous trepidation. She had been sitting upon pins and needles, as old Dorothy Stone would have expressed it, ever since Mr. Wade had been shut in with Miss Winter. The inspector noted her aspect, and took the bull by the horns. He did not say to her: "Madam, have you mentioned the fact to any one that such jewels were found?" He said, "To whom did you mention it?"

Her colour went and came; her heart was beating; her trembling fingers could not hold the needle--for she had some wool-work in her hands.

"I am afraid that I have been very thoughtless and foolish," she began, with a quaver of the voice. "Of course, I quite understood that no mention of the jewels was to be made in presence of any of the domestics, but it never struck me that the prohibition was intended to be a general one. You may remember, my dear Miss Winter, that I went to The Lilacs, in your place, on Thursday afternoon, to the tea-party. And--and, somehow--we ladies were all talking together; one topic led to another--and----"

Mrs. Toynbee broke down, from sheer nervousness.

"And you told of the finding of the jewels, and where they were deposited," spoke up the inspector.

"It was led up to," she said, excusing her self in the best way she could, and hardly able to keep from tears. "The ladies had been saying to me that I must find a country life very much lacking in excitement, after the metropolis; to which I replied that we were not always destitute of excitement, even in the country; and I--I then did speak of the jewels. But who was to imagine," she added, plucking up a little spirit, "that even the smallest danger could exist in mentioning it among ladies? They are all well-known; as trustworthy as we are."

"Do I gather, madam, that only ladies were present?" said the inspector. "No gentlemen?"

"It was a meeting for ladies only," replied Mrs. Toynbee. "One gentleman came in towards the last--Mr. Philip Cleeve. He came to fetch his mother. I remember he made a remark to the effect that the bureau was not a very safe place to leave the jewels in."

"A very sensible remark to make, under the circumstances," returned the inspector, drily. "Madam, can you give me the names of the ladies who were present?"

"Oh yes," replied Mrs. Toynbee; "we were not many--eight or ten, or so." And she succeeded in remembering all the names.

They were all well-known gentlewomen--all trustworthy, as the inspector had reason to know and believe.

"One of them must have mentioned it abroad, in the hearing of some dangerous ears," he said to himself. "Madam," he added, aloud, to Miss Winter, "I will not detain you further at present; but it may be necessary to see you again."

"Whenever you will, Mr. Wade," she sighed. "It is a dreadful thing altogether--and very mysterious. It seems to me that we have had nothing but painful mysteries for some time now at Heron Dyke."

The chief-constable glanced rather keenly at Miss Winter, in answer to this, and took his leave. As he closed the drawing-room door Mrs. Toynbee's suppressed tears burst forth.

"I am heartbroken, my dear," she sobbed--and, in truth, she did seem bitterly repentant: "perfectly heartbroken to think that any thoughtless remarks of mine should have conduced in any way to this terrible catastrophe. I never thought that anything I might say in a moment of confidence----"

"I should not have thought there was much danger in it myself," interrupted Miss Winter, kindly. "Do not distress yourself. They must have talked of it again, you see; and so it must have got about, and come to the knowledge of improper people."

"Oh dear!" wailed Mrs. Toynbee. "Yes, that is how it must have been. I wish I had known nothing about the jewels!"

Leaving her to her repentant sorrow, Ella went to see after poor Mrs. Stone.

Dorothy--she knew the worst now--was in her own sitting-room, leaning back in an easy-chair before a good fire, attired in her Sunday gown and cap--a soft black twill, trimmed handsomely with crape; a cap of white net and black gauze ribbon--for they were yet in deep mourning for the Squire. Perhaps some vague idea of its being a sort of holiday for the old woman would do no work that day--had induced her to put these best things on.

At Dorothy's age the outward signs of great emotions last but for a little while. Tears may come, but they do not flow so plentifully as in youth: the springs are deeper down, and more difficult to reach, and when found are sometimes almost dry. As age creeps on, and one or other of our loved ones drops silently from our side, it seems but such a little time till we hope to see them again, the period of separation is so short, as they are we ourselves shall so soon be, that we cannot mourn their loss with that intensity which we should have felt in youth, when the plains before us stretched to a limitless horizon, and our heartstrings were responsive to the slightest touch.

The young mistress sat down beside Dorothy, and took one of the old woman's withered hands between her own. That soft, warm, caressing touch unsealed again the fountains of the aged heart. With her other hand she lifted a corner of her apron to her eyes. For a minute or two neither of them spoke.

"What a handsome, brave lad he was, Miss Ella!" cried Dorothy at length. "Fit to be a lord's son, any day; and with as bold and masterful a spirit as any gentleman need wish to have: and now to think of him lying there, white and cold and dumb--he that had a laugh and a ready word for everybody. Alack! alack! if I could but be lying there instead of him!"

"My poor Dorothy! I do indeed feel for you."

"I knew when I saw the headless horses and the black coach that night in the park that there would be a death among us before long," she continued; "but I little thought my own bright boy would be the one to go. Ah! we never know; we never know. Though he was ill that night with his throat; and that might have whispered to me that the apparition was for him."

"Dorothy, do not dwell upon such things."

"Miss Ella, trust an old woman who has had a vast experience of life. Such signs and tokens are not sent for nothing, though some folks may laugh at you for heeding them. They are warnings from another world," added the old woman solemnly, "and some day it may be made plain to us why they are sent."

An inquest was held; some evidence was taken; and then it was adjourned for a week that the police might have time to make further investigations. They could not, as yet, learn that one suspicious person had known of the jewels.

Of all Miss Winter's friends, the one to make himself most busy was the Vicar of Nullington. An idle, easy-going man in general, Mr. Kettle could be aroused in a case like this: all his sympathies were with Miss Winter, and his curiosity was on the alert.

"After all," he observed to that young lady, one day when he was sitting with her to discuss details, "after all, the most mysterious part of the affair is not the sudden appearance of Hubert Stone on the scene. I daresay he could readily account for that, poor fellow, if he were living; perhaps he got in by the mail-train on the Sunday night, which you know passes at nearly one o'clock in the morning, and did not care to knock people up. No, the mystery lies in how the information, as to the hiding-place of the jewels, reached the cognisance of the rogue who stole them. And really, as Chief-Constable Wade justly observed, it would seem next to a certainty that the thief must be someone who had an intimate knowledge of the premises of Heron Dyke. You must see that, my dear, for yourself."

"I fear I do," sighed Ella.

"So far as people's recollection serves, Mrs. Toynbee mentioned simply that the bureau had been removed to your morning-room: Miss Winter's morning-room. Now, how should a common thief know which was Miss Winter's morning-room? It is only since the Squire died and your return that you have made it such."

"True," assented Ella.

"And altogether, taking one thing with another, I feel inclined to think it might have been no common thief who took them."

Ella lifted her eyes quickly. "Have you any suspicions?--of any one in particular?"

"No, my dear; no," he answered slowly; and, she thought, dubiously. "We can but wait. Perhaps Wade may ferret out more particulars."

But, on the same evening, when the Vicar was at home, safe within the four walls of his study, he dropped a word or two that nearly scared his daughter out of her senses. Somehow he had caught up a doubt in his own mind of Philip Cleeve.

"Oh, papa!" exclaimed Maria, in an accent of indignant horror.

"I don't say it was he, Maria; I should be very sorry to do that, or to breathe a syllable of this doubt to any one but you. Still, I cannot shut my eyes to the fact that things with regard to Philip do look somewhat suspicious--and Dr. Downes has long thought the same."

"Papa, papa!" she repeated.

"See here, child. In all the mysterious robberies that have taken place, and puzzled us for the past eighteen months, Philip has been present, beginning with Mrs. Carlyon's jewels. He was at her house the evening they were stolen; he was with Downes when he lost his snuff-box--he was with me when my purse disappeared. And, egad, if you come to that," added the Vicar, speaking rather unguardedly in his heat of recollection, "he was with Lennox and Freddy Bootle in London the night they lost things--the one his watch, the other his money."

"This is dreadful," gasped Maria. "Papa, it is not true; it cannot be. I would answer for Philip with my life."

"Very unwise of you, my dear. I have not finished. When that ridiculous woman up yonder"--pointing his finger in the direction of Heron Dyke--"blurted out the story of the jewels at Mrs. Ducie's, and where they were deposited, Philip Cleeve heard her; he was the only man present. I don't accuse him, I say, Maria, but I cannot get these truths out of my mind."

And, for answer, Maria burst into a flood of distressed tears.

The funeral of Hubert Stone took place, and was attended by half the population of Nullington. Old Aaron was chief mourner. On the coffin lay a wreath of exquisite flowers, placed there, before it left the Hall, by the hands of one by whom the past had been forgiven.

A day or two later the jury met again. Nothing fresh had been discovered. The police found out that Hubert Stone had come by train from London on the Saturday; he had stayed at a small inn a mile or two away until the Sunday evening, and had then gone out. From that hour he had never been seen alive, so far as could be traced.

The verdict returned was wilful murder against some person or persons unknown. Rewards were offered for any discovery; one by Miss Winter, another by Government.

Dr. Spreckley had taken an opportunity of giving to Miss Winter the likeness he had taken from Hubert's locket. "So foolish of the young man," he lightly remarked: "but I fancy he had as great a reverence for you, his mistress, as he had for the Squire."

"Yes," said Ella. "Thank you. Thank you very much, dear Dr. Spreckley," she earnestly added. And she put the bit of card-board in the fire there and then.

Ella had some intimate friends living close to Norwich: the Cursitors. Old Colonel Cursitor, he was hale and hearty yet, and the Squire had been companions in early life. Some of them came over and insisted upon carrying Ella back with them for a week. And she was glad to yield; to get away. Mrs. Toynbee took the opportunity to get away also, and went to stay with her sister in London.

This need not have been mentioned, but for a little matter that occurred during their absence. The servant girl, Betsy Tucker, was taken ill. Her symptoms were those of fever, and old Aaron protested that she should be got out of the house. "A pretty thing if the Hall is to be filled with typhus and what not!" he growled--for Hubert's death did not seem to have sweetened his temper. "A nice sort of wind-up that would be!"

"Let her come to me," cried Mrs. Keen, briskly, in whose hearing this was said; the landlady having gone to the Hall to see the girl. "I am not afraid it's going to be any thing infectious; I don't think it is. I knew her mother, you may remember, Mr. Stone."

Aaron closed with the offer at once. And the first news that greeted the mistress of Heron Dyke, returning from her week's visit to the pleasant city of Norwich, was that Betsy Tucker was ill of fever; and that she had been sent out of the house by Aaron, to get well, or die, at the "Leaning Gate."

Miss Winter showed herself to be very angry at the removal. But the thing was done.

CHAPTER II.

WHAT PRISCILLA PEYTON HAD TO TELL

In a cheerful room at Heron Dyke, with the morning sun shining upon it, there sat two young women, busily plying their needles: Miss Winter's maid, Adèle, and a dressmaker, one Priscilla Peyton. Priscilla was a homely, pleasant-featured person, between thirty and forty, who had often been employed at the Hall. They were making a morning gown for the Hall's mistress.

"What am I to do?" suddenly cried Priscilla. "It is impossible to get on without cord. I thought you would be sure to have some up here, or I'd have brought it with me."

"We generally do have it--plenty of it, but it was all used up last week, Miss Peyton," replied Adèle; a steady, dark young woman, who spoke English and French equally well.

Miss Winter came into the room at this juncture, and the difficulty was revealed to her. She said Adèle had better go to the nearest shop, one at this end of Nullington, and buy some cord.

But to this order the dressmaker looked as if she would like to demur. "What is it, Priscilla?" asked Miss Winter. "Can you not spare her?"

"Well, ma'am, the truth is, I shall be waiting for that frilling she is hemming."

"Oh, I will finish that for you, Priscilla," readily replied the young lady, who had a natural aptitude and liking for work.

She took a seat by the window; and Adèle departed in search of what was required. Hemming quickly at the strip of cambric, Ella talked the while to Priscilla Peyton, whom she had known--and esteemed--for years.

"It is some time since you were at work here, is it not, Priscilla?" she remarked.

"Well, it is, ma'am. With so many more maids in the house, Mrs. Stone gets done for her what I used to come to do. The last time I was here at work was when you were abroad, Miss Ella, and the poor Squire was lying ill."

"Did you see him?"

"Oh no, ma'am: oh no. Nobody used to see him then, save the doctor, and that. I was here the best part of a week, mending gowns for Mrs. Stone, and making her a new one. It was only about a fortnight before the Squire died."

Ella sighed. Priscilla Peyton, bending over her work, spoke again.

"I used to think, sitting in Mrs. Stone's parlour, how much I should like to see him once again; yes, I did, ma'am. I said so one day to Eliza; and she answered me that I might just as well wish to see the inside of the moon--that for months and months nobody had been admitted to see the Squire but those that had the pass-keys."

Ella, looking up from her work, stared at the neat brown hair and the neat white cap of the young woman, bending over hers, as if she were asking some solution to the words.

"Pass-keys?" she repeated. "What were they?"

"Keys that would open the green baize doors which the Squire had put up to shut out his rooms from the rest of the house, and which were always kept locked night and day, ma'am," replied Priscilla.

"And who kept these pass-keys?"

"There were four of them, ma'am," Priscilla said, "and four people had them, one each. Aaron Stone and poor Mr. Hubert, who is just gone; Dr. Jago had one, and the nurse."

Ella paused. "Of what nurse do you speak? My uncle never had a nurse."

"Indeed he had, Miss Ella. It was a Mrs. Dexter: sent for from London by Dr. Jago."

A nurse from London! This was the first time Miss Winter had heard of the existence of such a person at the Hall. The revelation was not palatable to her.

"How long was this Mrs. Dexter at the Hall--do you know, Priscilla?"

"It was a good while, ma'am; though I can't say exactly. I think she was here before Christmas--I am next to sure of it. Why yes--I remember now," quickly added the young woman; "she came in November. I was up here one wet November day; and while I was drying my petticoats at the kitchen fire, Phemie whispered to me that she thought the master must be worse, for they had got a London nurse in the house."

"Did this nurse remain with my uncle till the last?"

"She did, ma'am. She left the day after his death, in May."

Miss Winter said no more; she was thinking. Why was the presence of this nurse in the house kept from her?--for kept it assuredly had been. Why and wherefore had the woman's name never been mentioned to her, or the fact of her having been so long at the Hall? Her uncle had not spoken of her in his letters, or Hubert Stone in his notes.

"I saw Mrs. Dexter take her departure," resumed Priscilla, as a bit of gossip. "A lovely May morning it was, and I had gone to the station to see my little nephew off by the London train. Mrs. Dexter drove up in a fly, with a trunk and a little black bag that she carried in her hand, and I saw her get into the train. It was but the day after the Squire died; the bells were tolling for him."

And of course but two or three days before Miss Winter's return. And yet no one inmate of the Hall had informed her that this nurse had been there! It was altogether very strange.

"Did you say, Priscilla, that people at the last were not admitted to see my uncle, save those who had the pass-keys?"

"Ma'am, not for months and months. Eliza told me she did not believe a soul had been allowed to go in to see him since the past November. No matter who came--the Reverend Mr. Kettle, or any other of the Squire's old friends, they were never let go in."

"I wonder why?" involuntarily exclaimed Miss Winter.

"That I couldn't say, ma'am. Nobody could, I expect, save Dr. Jago. It must have been frightfully lonely for him, poor sick gentleman! He was never seen at all, or his footsteps heard, or the sound of his voice, Eliza said. To the girl it seemed just as though he were shut up in a living tomb."

Miss Winter asked no more questions. That something, and of set purpose, had been hidden from her; some drama enacted within those walls of which it was intended that she should know nothing, she fully believed. And there came rushing into her mind Hubert Stone's words--that if the truth were known she was no more the owner of Heron Dyke than he was. Again and again she asked herself what the truth was, and how it could be brought to light.

Ella carried her trouble to Mr. Kettle, her uncle's friend of many years. She sat with him in his study, Maria being present. She revealed to him her doubts; she hinted at Hubert's strange assertion on the wreck; she repeated what Priscilla Peyton had said, and then she appealed to him to advise her what she ought to do next.

The Vicar was not remarkable for penetration or sagacity, but he was a kindly, well-disposed man where his own ease and comfort were not in question; and if his words were sometimes weak and ineffective, he could, when required, put on a very wise and solemn air, which in itself was a comfort to those who sought his advice. But he really did not see what advice he could give now.

"I was, myself," he said, "more surprised and hurt than I can tell you that for some months before my old friend's death I was denied all access to him--I, who had been in the habit of calling at the Hall at least once a fortnight, ay, and oftener, for the last twenty years. When I found myself rebuffed one time after another, I could hardly believe that it was the Squire's own personal wish that I should not see him, although they assured me it was so. Old Aaron would usher me into a room with as much politeness as he was in the habit of showing to anybody, and would take in my message. Back he would come; or else Dr. Jago, or that sly-looking, smooth-tongued nurse, or perhaps Hubert Stone. But, no matter who came, each had the same tale to tell. The Squire had had a worse night than usual, or he was asleep, or he was too weak to-day to see anyone; whatever the excuse might be, I was never allowed to see him. It was the source of very considerable pain to me at the time, and I expressed myself rather strongly about it in my letters to Maria."

"There *must* have been something in all this--don't you think so, sir?" returned Ella. "Something to conceal."

"It seems like it, my dear; it used to seem like it to me. But I do not see what it could be; and I am sure I cannot imagine anything that could tend to peril your inheritance."

"Nor I," said Ella, "I wish I could. I mean I wish I could see any solution by which these doubts could be set at rest. The will was quite in order; Mr. Daventry tells me so----"

"Having been drawn up by Mr. Daventry, you may be sure of that, my dear," interrupted the Vicar.

"The only one thing, he says, that could possibly render it invalid, is my uncle having died before his birthday," continued Ella.

"And we know he did not die before it. He lived nearly a month after it."

"I--suppose--he--did live?" spoke Ella, with much hesitation.

"Did live!" echoed the Vicar, in surprise. "Why of course he did. People saw him and spoke with him. Don't you know that the other Mr. Denison's lawyer and his clerk came to the Hall two or three days subsequently to the Squire's birthday, and had an interview with him?--saw him; conversed with him. How could they have done that had he not been living? The Squire went into one of his passions, it was said, dashed his beef-tea, cup and all, into the fire, and abused the lawyer to his face."

Ella could not help a smile.

"Yes," she said, "I was told of that."

"Then, what else is there to fear? For anyone to come to you and say that if certain facts were known to the world you would not be mistress of Heron Dyke, seems to me sheer nonsense--if not malice. Were I in your place, my dear Miss Winter, I should certainly trouble myself no further in the matter."

Ella shook her head.

"All these arguments seem so cogent, so true--and yet I cannot feel satisfied. I am at a loss to know what more to do."

"Do nothing," said the Vicar, decisively. "I think you attach an exaggerated importance to the words. Some designing rascal it must have been who spoke them--wanting to swindle money out of you. Give him into custody should he apply again."

Remembering how impossible it was that he could apply again, a sad shade passed over Ella's countenance. The Vicar saw it: and of course mistook it. He knitted his brow.

"Take my advice, my dear Miss Winter, and rest satisfied," he said. "Do not try to create a mystery where none exists, save in your own imagination."

There was no more to be said. The Vicar's reasoning and advice had been much like Mr. Daventry's. Ella wished she could feel as secure as they felt.

She and Maria went out together. They were going to the Leaning Gate. As it was now decided that the fever of Betsy Tucker was not an infectious one, and as the girl was said to be getting weaker, Miss Winter considered it was her duty to go to see her. Maria had been more than once.

"What do you think, Maria, of the advice your father gave me--to let this doubt as to my inheritance rest, and be satisfied?" questioned Ella, as they walked along. "Oh that I could see my way to a little more light!"

"Light does not always come when we ask for it, or when we fancy that we need it most," answered Maria, "and yet it generally comes at the time that is best for us. You must hope that it will do so in the present case: that is, if you still feel there is something hidden that you ought to know."

"That is just the feeling which I cannot get rid of. Were you in my place, Maria, what would you do?"

"I hardly know," answered Maria, slowly. "It seems to me that you are bound to leave no stone unturned in your efforts to discover the truth, and this none the less, perhaps indeed rather the more, that the truth, when revealed, may prove disastrous to you from a worldly point of view."

"I can only wait for more light," said Ella, with a sigh. "The difficulty is, how to get the light--where to look for it."

"I perceive that," said Maria. "You can but wait and watch. Here we are!--and there's poor Mrs. Keen."

Betsy Tucker was in bed, the victim of a distressing kind of low fever. Dr. Spreckley hoped to bring her through it, but he was not sanguine. After turning and tossing for hours incessantly, Mrs. Keen informed them she had now sunk into a troubled sleep. They stood by the bed in silence, looking at the sick girl's crimson-fevered cheeks.

"She is light-headed at times," whispered the landlady, "fancying herself back at the Hall. She starts up in bed, ma'am"--turning to Miss Winter--"crying out, 'Hush! there are the footsteps in the corridor again! And now,' she'll go on, 'they are trying the door. See! see! the handle moves!' and with that, ma'am, she sinks back on the pillow and buries her head under the clothes. For my part," concluded Mrs. Keen, "I cannot help thinking it was that night's fright which has brought on the fever."

"To what do you allude?" asked Miss Winter. "Has she been frightened?"

"Why yes, ma'am. But I thought you knew of it, or I'd not have spoken. It was talked of a good deal at the Hall. She was badly frightened."

"In what way?"

"It was the night of the storm a few weeks ago," replied the landlady, vexed to have alluded to this before Miss Winter, as it seemed she did not know of it. "Betsy could not get to sleep for the noise; and between the gusts of wind, when all was momentarily still, she heard footsteps walking about the corridor outside her bedroom door. After a time she struck a light, and then, so she says, she distinctly saw the handle of her room door turn this way and that, as though somebody was trying to get in; but she had locked it on going to bed. She came down here to tell me of it the next day, and I tried to persuade her that it was nothing more than her own idle fancies that had frightened her, till at last she got quite out of temper with me. It must have taken great hold of her mind, I'm afraid, by the way she talks of it in her wanderings now."

"I never heard anything of this," remarked Miss Winter. "But I cannot understand why Betsy need have been so much frightened. She might have guessed that the footsteps were but those of one or other of the maids, unable to sleep for the storm. And what more natural than that they should turn the handle of her door, intending to keep Betsy company?"

"Yes, ma'am," assented Mrs. Keen, looking down.

"If I were to allow myself to be frightened by all the unaccountable noises I hear in the night at the Hall, especially when the wind is high, I should never care to sleep there again," continued Miss Winter. "I have no doubt that all old houses are alike in that respect, especially when many of the rooms are empty."

"Where is Susan?" interposed Maria, breaking the pause of silence.

"She is gone out to do some errands, Miss Maria. Susan is a famous help to me in nursing Betsy."

"Susan was always very gentle and patient," remarked Ella.

"And always will be, I hope, ma'am," responded Mrs. Keen. "She is a girl that has very little to say for herself, as you know, young ladies. On most points she seems as sensible as other people are, but now and then her mind seems to go vacant, just as if it couldn't quite grasp what you are telling her; and her memory is not always to be trusted. But she's a dear good girl in helping me in the house; I don't know what I should do without her."

"Does her sister's disappearance seem to prey upon her mind as much as it used to do?" and Miss Winter unconsciously lowered her voice as she put the question.

"I don't believe it is ever out of her thoughts," answered the landlady. "I know quite well what Susan is thinking about when she sits perfectly still, as she will sometimes do for half-an-hour together, staring straight before her, but without seeing anything. Katherine's name is never mentioned in her presence now. I think it best," continued Mrs. Keen, her eyes filling with tears: "though Heaven knows, my poor lost darling is rarely out of my thoughts."

"You will of course see that Betsy Tucker wants for nothing, Mrs. Keen," said Miss Winter, as the landlady attended the young ladies to the door. "I was very much vexed, as I have already told you, that she should have been sent away from the Hall: she should not have been had I been at home. Everything requisite for her shall be sent to her from my house, and one of the maids shall come this evening to watch by her for the night. We must not have you laid up."

"Oh, ma'am, please don't think of me. I am strong, and used to work. All my anxiety is lest we should not bring her through."

"Dr. Spreckley assures me that he has still good hopes of her. And he is, you know, skilful and attentive."

Ella glanced at the little garden as they left the door. That which had looked so bright and pleasant in the summer had now little to show in the faint November sunshine but bare branches, empty beds, and footpaths strewed with withered leaves.

"I think Mrs. Keen must be mistaken in fancying Betsy Tucker's illness has arisen from the fright she got the night of the storm," observed Miss Winter, after they had walked some little time in silence. "It is incredible that the mere hearing of footsteps in the corridor, and seeing her door tried, should have terrified her to any extent. Her own sense ought to have told her that what she heard was merely the footsteps of some of the other maids who could not rest on account of the storm."

"The girl was very much frightened at the time, I believe," said Miss Kettle; "though there can be little doubt the impression would have worn off but for something which she unfortunately heard a day or two later. Two of the others were conversing about it, not knowing that she was within hearing; they said to one another that it must have been the ghost walking at night-- the ghost of Katherine Keen."

Miss Winter's brow knit angrily. "Who were those servants?"

"Eliza and Phemie. They had carefully kept it from the girl; and her hearing it was quite an accident. Betsy, it appears, believes in ghosts; and she confessed to Mrs. Keen she had never had one proper night's rest since, from fright."

"I suppose Mrs. Keen told you this, Maria?"

"Yes. The first time I went to see Betsy."

Miss Winter sighed. "I do not see what help there is for it. The whole affair remains as unaccountable as ever it was."

"Unaccountable, indeed," replied Maria, gravely. "At times when speaking of it, or hearing it spoken of, I turn shivery, as if I believed in the ghost myself. Here comes Susan."

The young girl, pleasant and placid-looking, was advancing with a basket of marketings. They stopped to speak to her. Miss Winter told her she was going to send one of the maids down to sit up with Betsy, and was passing onwards, when the anxious, appealing look in the girl's wan face arrested her.

"Did you wish to ask anything, Susan?"

"Oh, ma'am, if I might!--if I might!"

"Certainly you may. What is it?"

"I want to find out where they took Katherine to," spoke the girl in an urgent whisper. "Perhaps you know, ma'am; you are the mistress; and whether she is alive or dead."

"My poor Susan, I know no more about it than you do. I wish I did."

Susan clasped her hands, "I wonder how much longer we shall have to wait?"

"It may be, Susan, that we shall never know. It may be intended that we shall not know."

Susan shook her head. "I think it will all be known by-and-by, ma'am. Perhaps I shall be the one to find it out. I often wake up in the night and hear Katherine calling to me, only I can't tell where the voice comes from. I hear it oftenest in the larch plantation at the back of the Hall when the moon is at the full. But when I try to follow her voice I get bewildered with the strange fancies that seem to be dancing and whirling in my head; and sometimes I hear a laugh close behind me, and then I hurry off home and go to bed, and repeat hymns one after another till I get to sleep."

"There, run home now, Susan: your mother is waiting for you," interposed Miss Kettle with authority--for it was always best to cut off promptly these dreamy visions of Susan.

Ever obedient, Susan hastened towards the Leaning Gate, the far-away, spiritual expression dying out of her eyes. The others walked on, Maria with her gaze on the ground.

"Look opposite, Maria. There is some one you know."

Maria looked across the road, and saw Philip Cleeve, who appeared to be just as much absorbed as they were, his head bent in deep thought. He looked like Philip grown twenty years older--Philip without his elastic tread, his quick walk, his cheerful smile and greeting for everyone whom he knew. Not until he had nearly passed did he perceive Miss Winter and Maria. Happening to raise his eyes, he started, hesitated, flushed to the roots of his hair, lifted his hat, and hurried on.

Maria, too, flushed painfully, and a grieved look came into her eyes as she gravely acknowledged Philip's salutation, and walked on by Miss Winter's side.

"You and Philip have not quarrelled I hope, Maria?"

"Quarrelled--no," answered Maria with a sigh. "But he does not come to the Vicarage now; papa has forbidden it."

"He looks changed somehow."

"So I think. He spends, I believe, too much time in the billiard-room, and report talks of high play at The Lilacs with Lord Camberley and others. All these things distress me greatly."

"Naturally--if you feel a special interest in him," remarked Ella.

Again Maria's colour deepened.

"Just before I went to Leamington he asked me to be his wife."

"Did you refuse him?"

"For the time being."

"And you have not yet made up your mind to accept him?"

"No. How can I? I could never make up my mind unless papa's will went with it."

"Perhaps Philip is vexed--disheartened: and so flies to these foolish courses?"

"I don't know," sighed Maria. "It would show great weakness of mind, would it not?"

"People in love are said to be not always accountable for their actions. Poor Philip! But you love him still?"

"I never quite knew till lately what he is to me," answered Maria, in a low voice. "I have tried not to care for him, but----"

"You find that you, too, are a little weak-minded?"

"I suppose so. But he never passed me in the street before without speaking."

CHAPTER III.

MALACHITE AND GOLD

Of all days in the week, Saturday was the one most longed for by Ella Winter. The reason was that it always--or nearly always, for now and then there was a breakdown or a delay somewhere--brought her a letter from Edward Conroy. These letters were her greatest comfort in her perplexities and troubles. She read them and re-read them till she knew all their sweetest passages by heart. How she longed for his return that she might tell him everything!--for in truth she sometimes felt that the burden laid upon her was almost more than she could bear without help. Were he but here to share it with her! Absence had enabled her to read her heart in all its entirety, had endeared his image to her more day by day. Mr. Conroy was not expected in England until spring; but towards the end of November there came a letter, the contents of which filled his mistress with unexpected delight. Conroy's mission in Spain was nearly at an end, and he might be expected home in three or four weeks--in time, it might be, to eat his Christmas dinner. He did not tell her that latterly her letters had filled him with so much uneasiness that he had requested his employers to relieve him of his duties abroad, or that he had wisely made up his mind to ascertain for himself, and as quickly as possible, the exact state of affairs at Heron Dyke.

Little by little the popular excitement in connection with the murder and robbery at Heron Dyke began to subside, especially as all the efforts of the police resulted in no fresh discoveries. People had talked and wondered till there was nothing left to talk and wonder about. Fresh topics and other interests began to claim their attention. The newspapers had ceased to comment on the case, and there seemed every probability of its adding one more to the long list of undiscovered crimes.

One day Mrs. Toynbee, who had been shopping in the town, brought home a piece of news. Some one had told her that Dr. Jago was about to leave Nullington, the reason for his departure being that he had bought a more lucrative practice elsewhere. This set Ella thinking. Would it not be well, she asked herself, to see this man before he went away, and try whether she could not elicit from him something of that which she wanted to know? He had attended her uncle to the last; he must be acquainted with all that took place inside Heron Dyke during the time she was away; if any fraud had been at work it could hardly have been kept a secret from him. She disliked Dr. Jago, but it seemed to her that she ought not to let him go away without seeking an interview with him.

Next morning she finally made up her mind; so the pony-chaise was ordered round, and she was driven into Nullington. Calling at the Vicarage on her way, she took Miss Kettle into her confidence.

"Am I doing right, Maria, think you?"

"Yes, I think you are."

"Then you must accompany me. You have no objection?"

"Not the least in the world."

Dr. Jago was at home; and the young ladies, leaving the carriage with the groom, were shown into his consulting-room. Turning round from a case he was packing, the doctor changed colour, as if from annoyance, when he saw his visitors. The transitory expression passed, however; he greeted them civilly, apologising for the disorder of the place, and invited them to sit.

"I hear that you are about to quit Nullington, Dr. Jago," began Miss Winter, as she took the chair he placed.

"True, madam," he replied. "I have purchased a more lucrative practice in London. What can I have the honour of doing for you?"

"I have called to ask you a few questions, Dr. Jago. I hope you will be able to answer them."

The Doctor bowed.

"I was abroad, as you are aware, at the time my uncle died," she began; "but you saw him, I believe, in your medical capacity, up to the day of his death?"

"Yes," he replied. "I saw Mr. Denison daily; and I was with him when he died."

"The end, when it did come, was very sudden."

"Both sudden and unexpected," returned the Doctor. "I was utterly taken by surprise. I knew, of course, that Mr. Denison's disorder could have but one termination, but I had no thought that the end was so near. The heart suddenly failed in its action, and--and all was over. Only a few hours before, when I was with him, I had detected no cause for fear."

"You are aware that previously to last Christmas--in October I think it was--Dr. Spreckley, who had attended my uncle for twenty years, and who ought to have known his constitution if it were possible for anyone to know it, gave it as his decided opinion that Mr. Denison could not live far into the new year--if so long as that."

"Mr. Denison himself informed me of that opinion."

"And yet your skill prolonged his life until nearly the end of May?"

Dr. Jago bowed again, but said nothing.

"Then you, although a much younger practitioner than Dr. Spreckley, must have pursued a very much more efficient mode of treatment with your patient than that adopted by him?"

Dr. Jago shrugged his shoulders, leaned forward in his chair, and smiled faintly. "I have not the slightest wish in the world to disparage Dr. Spreckley," he said, "but it may be that he is a little old-fashioned in his ideas; it may be that he has hardly grown with the times. Medicine has made great strides during the last twenty years, and a middle-aged country practitioner, unless he be a great reader and a man of inquiring mind, would find many things taught, and many theories demonstrated in the schools of London and Paris, which were hardly as much as mooted when he was a young man."

All this seemed only fair and reasonable. In any case, Miss Winter was not prepared to refute it. She paused for a moment or two before she spoke again.

"It may or it may not have come to your notice, Dr. Jago," she said, eyeing him steadily as she spoke, "that there are certain reports flying about the neighbourhood--reports unpleasant to all concerned, but which you could no doubt put an end to if you chose to do so."

"Reports! About what, Miss Winter?" he asked quickly.

Ella paused: it seemed somewhat difficult to frame words for what she wanted to say.

"I hardly know how to put it," she said with a frank smile. "People have in some way picked up a notion that there was some deceit or fraud at work in connection with my uncle's death."

"Oh, have they?" was all the answer the Doctor made, speaking carelessly.

"It is said that for some months before Mr. Denison died he was immured away from everyone except three or four people; that he was kept under lock and key; that all his old friends were denied access to him. Also, that at the very time my letters from home informed me he was growing stronger day by day and week by week, a strange woman, some London nurse, was in the house, in regular attendance on him. People naturally ask why there should have been all this mystery unless there was something to hide. They even go so far as to hint that the master of Heron Dyke did not live to see his seventieth birthday."

Dr. Jago, despite his evident efforts, could not avoid changing countenance as Miss Winter spoke. His face turned sallow; his eyes fell. Suddenly he rose and opened the door.

"Is that you, James?" he called out. But no one answered.

"I beg your pardon," he said, resuming his seat, and quite calm now, "I thought I heard my servant knock. About this business, Miss Winter. If one were to take heed of all the idle tales set afloat by ignorant and foolish people, one would have little else to do. The late Mr. Denison was an eccentric man in many ways, as you yourself must be well aware. He was a man of strong individuality and of crotchety temper; a man who did very few things in quite the same way as ordinary people do them. There were, besides, certain peculiar features in connection with the disposition of his property, which were well known in the neighbourhood, and which acted as a magnet to the curiosity of the world. These points being granted, we have at once a foundation for the most ridiculous fancies and the most exaggerated gossip; but if we quietly set ourselves to sift these rumours, what do we find?"

Ella did not speak.

"If you will allow me, Miss Winter, I will take the case as stated in your own words. You say that for some months before Mr. Denison died he was immured away from everyone except three or four people, and kept, as it were, under lock and key. Granted; but it was done entirely at his own request. You perhaps remember something of that queer crotchet he had in his head that the precincts of the Hall, and even the Hall itself, were haunted by spies set on to watch him by certain people--his relatives, I believe, but of that I know little. This notion seemed to take fuller hold of him as his birthday drew nearer. He insisted on having his rooms shut in from the rest of the house; he decreed that only a very few individuals, those whom he could implicitly trust, should have access to him. None of the ordinary servants were to go near him; for aught he knew, he would declare, they might be spies. It was an hallucination I combated as far as I was able; but contradiction, especially on this point, only irritated him. More than once it brought on one of his fits of passion, and so undid, or partially undid, the good I was striving to do him in other ways."

This was quite feasible, probably true, and Miss Winter bowed her head in acquiescence. The Doctor resumed.

"As regards Mr. Denison's old friends being denied access to him, I must take on myself a certain measure of blame for what may seem a somewhat arbitrary proceeding. From the first I gave Mr. Denison to understand that if he adopted my mode of treatment, perfect quiet and seclusion were essential to its success, and he agreed with me without the slightest demur.

But I did not at first deny him the sight of friends: it was only after the visits of some of them, when I saw how much it excited him, that I was obliged to do so. I begged him to allow his rooms to be closed to all visitors: had he admitted one he must have admitted others: I showed him how essential it was that he should be kept strictly, perfectly quiet; and he agreed. He would agree to anything, he said, if I could only succeed in keeping him alive over his seventieth birthday; and I certainly did succeed in doing that."

"Did he require the services of a nurse?"

"Undoubtedly."

"And was it necessary that she should be a stranger?"

"In my opinion he ought to have been supplied with a properly trained nurse long before I sent for one. An old woman, had in haphazard from the neighbourhood, would have been useless. No one, except we medical men and those invalids who have tried them, know how invaluable is a really qualified nurse in a sick-room."

"I believe that," said Ella, hastily. "But--why was it that the fact of this nurse having been at Heron Dyke was never mentioned to me? Neither in the letters I received from home, nor when I returned to it, close upon the departure of the nurse, was she as much as named to me."

Dr. Jago shook his head.

"I cannot enlighten you there," he answered. "*I* did not keep the fact from you. I neither wrote you letters nor saw you on your return. There could be no reason whatever, so far as I know, why you should not have been privy to it. What reason could there be? Possibly it may have been one of old Aaron's crotchets--for he had as many as his master--that you should not be told."

Possibly it had been: but Miss Winter still felt in a fog, plausible though all this was.

"Can you assure me, Dr. Jago, that the seeing one or two of his oldest friends would have been absolutely detrimental to my uncle? Say--for instance--the Vicar."

"Papa thought it very strange: he thinks it so still, that he was always denied admittance," interposed Maria, speaking for the first time. And the Doctor turned sharply to her with a slight frown, as though he had forgotten her presence.

"I cannot say it would have been fatally detrimental, but it might have been," he observed, in answer to Miss Winter. "He himself knew the danger of excitement, and he was as anxious as I was to guard against the possibility of it. With regard to the other report you have mentioned, Miss Winter--that Mr. Denison did not live over his seventieth birthday--it is, upon my word, too ridiculous a one to refute. Mr. Denison was seen by many people later and talked with--talked with face to face. Webb the lawyer saw him, and spoke with him about his will. Those other lawyers, men from London, had an interview with him. He was seen by no end of people, musicians and others, on his birthday night. In the face of these facts, how is it possible-- pardon me the remark, Miss Winter--for you to give ear for a moment to so absurd a rumour?"

She sat in thought, not answering.

"Where was the deception--where the fraud?" he resumed. "Indeed, where was the necessity for employing any? The great object of Mr. Denison's life was attained. He had outlived his seventieth birthday, and the property was his own to will away. Fraud! It is an assertion that brings with it its own contradiction."

There was nothing more to be said, nothing more, evidently, to be learned from Dr. Jago: and with civil adieux on both sides, the ladies took their departure, the Doctor attending them to the pony-carriage and handing them into it. At that moment Dr. Spreckley passed on horseback; he stared profoundly, as much as to say, "What on earth do you do at that man's house?"--and he almost forgot to salute them.

Miss Winter sat in deep thought as they drove away. That Dr. Jago had displayed nervousness, not to say agitation, when spoken to, she had not failed to observe; it had served to deepen her conviction that something was hidden which it was intended that she, of all people in the world, should never know. And although his assertions afterwards had seemed perfectly reasonable and convincing, she could not get rid of an uneasy suspicion that the Doctor, metaphorically speaking, had been throwing dust in her eyes. Any way, she was as far off as ever, if not farther, from arriving at the truth.

"What do you think of Dr. Jago?" she abruptly asked Maria.

"I don't like him at all, Ella. His words are plausible enough, indeed too plausible, but he seems thoroughly insincere. He is a man whom I should always mistrust. Have you questioned your servants?"

"Only old Aaron. And I can get nothing from him. His reasoning is in substance the same as Dr. Jago's. Maria, I feel *sure* that some trickery was at work."

"I should ask the maids, Phemie and Eliza, whether they noticed anything strange. They must have been about the house much during all the time."

"I think I will. It has crossed my mind to do so, but I feared they would only make my questions into a source of gossip."

Miss Kettle paused.

"Tell me exactly what it is that you suspect."

"I do not know what to suspect, except that I have a strong idea of some unfair play having been enacted. There lies my difficulty. But that it seems so impossible, and so dreadful an idea besides, I might say that my uncle did *not* live to see his birthday."

Maria shivered slightly.

"Oh, Ella!"

"It is the bent my fears are taking," whispered Miss Winter. "And in that case, you know, I am not the owner of Heron Dyke."

"No, no, Ella, I cannot believe that," said Maria. "Your fears are making you fanciful."

That same evening, Miss Winter had the two maids, Phemie and Eliza, before her, and questioned them of matters respecting the Squire's last illness. What they had to tell was little more than she had heard from Priscilla Peyton. For several weeks or months previously to the 24th April, no one in the house, except the four people who were admitted behind the green baize doors, ever saw or heard anything of the Squire.

"Had you reason to think he was *very* ill?" asked Miss Winter.

"Ma'am, we could tell nothing," replied Phemie. "He might have been dead and buried for weeks and weeks, for all we saw or heard of him. Eliza and I used to say how strange it was: often we listened, often and often, but never got to hear him; never so much as heard him cough. Before that Mrs. Dexter came in November, I sometimes took his sago or his beef-tea to him, but never afterwards."

"How was it that you never mentioned to me that Mrs. Dexter had been here? Was it accident?

"No, ma'am, it was Aaron;" and Miss Winter could not help smiling at the turn of the sentence. "The day before you were expected home, he ordered all in the house not to talk of Mrs. Dexter: he thought it might trouble you to hear that the Squire was so ill as to need a nurse from London."

"I suppose you never penetrated beyond the green baize doors, after they were put up?"

Phemie glanced at her fellow-servant.

"Eliza did, ma'am, once. You had better tell of it, Eliza."

"Tell me all, Eliza; do not be afraid," said Miss Winter kindly, for the girl looked confused.

"If you please, ma'am, I was in the passage one day, and saw both the doors on the jar," began Eliza. "I thought it no harm to go in a few steps; but I went cautiously, thinking Mr. Stone must be there. However, I saw nobody; and then I thought Mrs. Dexter must have left them open by mistake, before she went out. She had gone into Nullington in a hurry, saying she must see Dr. Jago."

"Well? Go on, Eliza."

"I ventured in a little farther, and a little farther," continued Eliza, speaking freely now. "Everything was silent. I said to myself that perhaps the Squire was asleep, and then I thought that I should like to see him once again. The first room I came to was Mrs. Dexter's; it had been made into a chamber for her. I turned the handle softly, pushed open the door, and peeped in. There was her bed in one corner, and by the fire-place was her little round table and an easy-chair. From this room I went to the next, which was Mr. Denison's sitting-room. The door opened without making any noise. I peeped in. There was no one there. The Squire's chair stood by the hearth, but it was empty, and there was no fire in the grate; it had the look of a room, ma'am, that had not been occupied for ever so long, and somehow I turned away with a chill at my heart. The next room was the Squire's bedroom. I don't think I should have ventured to open the door of this, but I found it open already. It was standing ajar. I listened for the sound of Mr. Denison's breathing, supposing that he was asleep, but I could hear nothing. Then I pushed the door a little further open and looked in. If you'll believe me, ma'am, he was not there. No one was there."

"He must have been somewhere in the room, Eliza."

"He was not, indeed, ma'am. The room was empty. I could hardly believe my eyes. I walked across it to the window and back again. The room was all tidy, like one that is not in use; not as much as a book was about, or a chair out of place. The bed was made and the curtains folded upon it."

This news sounded wonderful. Ella could not speak.

"I felt quite frightened, ma'am. I said to myself what has become of the master? and I can't fathom the mystery of where he could be, to this day."

"There was a room beyond my uncle's--a dark, unused room," spoke Miss Winter. "Did you enter that?"

"No, ma'am. I tried the door of it, but it was locked, and the key gone. But the Squire, ma'am, would not be in there--in a locked-up lumber-room. I said to Phemie afterwards----"

Eliza stopped suddenly and coloured. Her mistress bade her continue.

"Well, ma'am, when I was telling Phemie of this strange thing, I said to her that the thought had come over me when I saw the empty bed and no trace of him in the room, that it looked just as if the master had been spirited away like Katherine Keen."

To this Miss Winter said nothing.

"Was it discovered that you had been in?" she asked.

"No, ma'am, never; and this is the first time I have talked of it, except to Phemie. I pulled the baize doors to after me when I came out, and they shut with a snap. By-and-by, back came Mrs. Dexter; she asked at once in the kitchen for the Squire's beef-tea, and took it away with her. But, ma'am, what I cannot imagine is, where the Squire was all the time."

Miss Winter could not imagine, either, and lost herself in unfathomable conjecture. After a few more questions, she dismissed the maids, charging them not to speak of this.

The girl, Betsy Tucker, grew worse rather than better; and, notwithstanding all that skill and good nursing could do for her, Dr. Spreckley began to despair of her recovery. Miss Winter was startled one afternoon when Adèle came to her and said Mrs. Keen was asking to be admitted.

"Show her in, Adèle," said Miss Winter, in a low tone. She was afraid the girl was dead.

"No, ma'am, and I don't think she is any worse," replied the landlady, in answer to the dread question. "If anything, she's perhaps a little better. She don't wander quite so much, and that I take to be a good sign. What I have made bold to interrupt you about, Miss Ella, is another thing."

"Sit down while you tell it me," said Ella.

"Thank you, ma'am. This morning, Betsy, who was quite herself, though very weak, asked me to put the small trunk, which came with her from the Hall, upon the bed, so that she might find something," began Mrs. Keen, taking the chair indicated. "It was a pocket she wanted; and we were some time finding it, what with her hands being feeble and me not knowing what it was like--white or coloured. Out of the pocket, when we had found it, she drew this tiny packet, ma'am, and asked me would I take it myself up to the Hall and give it safely to Miss Winter?"

The little packet was neatly folded in tissue-paper, tied round with narrow pink ribbon. Ella, rather wonderingly, opened it. Amidst some folds of cotton wool lay a gentleman's sleeve-link. It was of malachite and gold, of curious and very uncommon workmanship. Miss Winter had never, to her knowledge, seen it before. "What is it?" she asked. "Why do you bring it to me, Mrs. Keen?"

The landlady explained. "Betsy's mind is in trouble about it, Miss Ella," she began; "in great trouble. It seems that the morning poor Hubert Stone was found, Betsy, after all was quiet, and the police and other people had gone, was outside there. She saw something shining on the gravel, and picked it up. It was this trinket; she thought it very lovely, she tells me; and on the impulse of the moment she picked it up and put it in her pocket, thinking it would be a pretty present for her sweetheart, who is no other than David Beal, the joiner's son. And I suspect, ma'am, though she has not said as much, that it was just to be near him she took a situation over here."

"Very possibly," assented Miss Winter. "But she ought not to have concealed or kept this."

"It is that which is tormenting her now, ma'am. She couldn't rest till I had brought it to you and told you all. The girl says, and I can but believe her, that in the night, when she was in bed, she saw the wrong she had done, and repented of it, but was afraid then of confessing. All kinds of foolish fancies visit us in the night, as you know, Miss Ella, and she says an idea came into her mind that if she confessed what she had done and produced the trinket, she might, perhaps, be accused of having been mixed up with the robbery. So she wrapped and tied it up, and has kept it hidden in her pocket till now. All her cry since she came into her right mind is, 'If Miss Winter will but forgive me!'"

"Yes, yes; tell her I forgive her, Mrs. Keen. It seems to me that when we do wrong, our own conscience brings to us our worst punishment. And I am truly glad that the girl is getting better: I will call and see her to-morrow. Have you disclosed this to anyone, or shown the link?"

"Indeed no, ma'am; not even to Susan. It was not my place to do so."

"Keep it quite secret still," said Ella. "For aught we can tell this link may afford some clue to elucidate what is, as yet, so dark."

The landlady took her leave, and Ella locked the trinket safely up for the present. On the following morning Mrs. Toynbee received a letter calling her away from Heron Dyke. Her sister in London had met with an accident, and begged her to come up for a few days, if she could be spared.

"Go by all means," said Ella, in answer to Mrs. Toynbee's tearful looks, as she put the letter into her hand. "Take the mid-day train. Lonely? Well, perhaps I should feel a little lonely under recent circumstances if left to myself; but I will get Maria Kettle to stay with me. It will do her good: she is anything but well."

Maria was suffering from the effects of a severe cold, caught one bitter night when returning home from visiting a sick pensioner. Ella drove to the Vicarage and brought her away. Maria would have said no, but her father said yes.

The next day she seemed not at all better, but very poorly and feverish. Whilst Ella was dressing for dinner Maria came to her room, asking to be excused from dining: she felt hardly well enough to go down, especially as they should not be alone.

Only Mr. Daventry would be there. Ella had met him that morning and invited him to come: she was uneasy about many things, and wanted to talk to him. "You shall lie down here, Maria," said she, pushing her dressing-room sofa close to the fire, "and have some tea sent up. Adèle shall get it for you."

Maria lay down on the sofa, wrapping a shawl about her head, and drank the tea. After that, she fell asleep. Ella was glad to hear it, as it left her evening free for Mr. Daventry.

The old lawyer took his departure at nine o'clock. For a few minutes Ella sat over the fire, musing on the advice he had given her--to be still for the present; not to take action on any point. From this reverie she was aroused by the sharp and sudden opening of the door. Maria Kettle stood there, staggering in, rather than walking, her face white, her eyes full of terror.

"Oh, Ella!" she gasped.

Ella sprang to her feet, her pulses quivering. "You are worse, Maria!" she cried, "sit down here."

"No, it is not that--not that," moaned Maria, sinking back in the large arm-chair, but recently vacated by Mr. Daventry. "I have seen Katherine Keen."

"Katherine Keen!" breathed Ella, her lips suddenly becoming dry. "Impossible!"

"I should have said the same myself ten minutes ago," returned the sick girl, as she strove for composure. "But when I tell you, Ella, that I have seen her, and that I am in possession of my senses, I think you must believe me."

Ella Winter shivered, as though a cold wind were passing over her. Kneeling down, she put her arm round Maria's waist. "Tell me about it," she whispered.

"I got warm after I had the tea, and soon fell fast asleep," said Maria, in a voice hushed and trembling. "I knew nothing more until I awoke, suddenly and completely, with the strange feeling, which most people have experienced at one time or another, that some one was bending over me. My eyes opened widely, as though of their own accord; and there, bending down and gazing earnestly into my face, was the face of Katherine Keen."

"Maria!"

"I recognised it in a moment. The room was bright with firelight, and I could not be mistaken. There was the fair hair, with the soft appealing eyes and the sad and serious look in them that I remember so well."

"Did you speak?"

"For a moment or two we gazed at each other; then I think my lips formed her name, but whether any sound came from them I cannot tell. The next thing I knew was that she was no longer there. I started up and saw a black-robed figure vanish through the open doorway and the door close noiselessly behind it. For an instant I thought I should have died."

"Black-robed," repeated Ella mechanically, remembering that this apparition had been always so described.

"She was in black from head to foot. Something black covered her head, which she held with the fingers of one hand under the chin. With her disappearance I sprang to the door, opened it, and rushed into the corridor."

"After her! You had courage, Maria."

"I had no courage. I was too terrified to remain alone, and was hastening to you. She was not to be seen; she had disappeared. A lamp was burning at the farther end of the passage, but the passage was quite empty, quite still; not a sound in it, save the beating of my own heart. Oh Ella! I have heard the mysteries of Heron Dyke spoken of, but I never thought to witness anything myself."

"Yes, Heron Dyke has no doubt its unhappy mysteries; has had them for some time now," sighed Ella, catching up her breath with a sob. "And I know not how to solve them."

CHAPTER IV.

MR. CHARLES PLACKETT IS PUZZLED

"Mind, Ella, you have promised to come to me in London during the autumn, and to stay for a fortnight at least," had been Mrs. Carlyon's last words to her niece when she was leaving Heron Dyke: and, in making the promise, Ella Winter had fully intended to fulfil it. But the autumn was drawing to a close, Christmas would be here before long, and the visit had not been paid. Circumstances had prevented it.

But in those circumstances there seemed to be a lull now; and Mrs. Carlyon took advantage of it. She wrote a pressing letter to Ella. The cold weather was setting in, she said, her cough was becoming troublesome, and she had nearly made up her mind to go to Hyères; but nothing would induce her to go anywhere, until she had seen her niece again.

By return of post Mrs. Carlyon received an answer. Ella would pay the visit at once. On the following day she and Maria Kettle, whom she begged leave to bring with her, would quit the Hall for Bayswater.

Change, as Miss Winter knew, would be good for Maria. It might not be amiss for herself. Truth to tell, Miss Winter had been more disturbed by her friend's positive assertion of having seen Katherine Keen, than she cared to acknowledge even to her own mind. Maria Kettle had a fund of practical good sense, she was not at all romantically inclined; and Ella could not pooh-pooh her account, strange though it might be, as she probably would have done that of an uneducated or superstitious person.

Maria's account did not stand alone: it was impossible for Miss Winter not to recall how strongly it was corroborated. She herself had never forgotten her visit to Katherine's room, when she found the face of the looking-glass so mysteriously covered up. There had followed the positive assertions of the two maids, Ann and Martha, that they had seen Katherine--and both of them had known her well--looking down at them over the balusters of the gallery. After that came Mrs. Carlyon's fright; although in her case no face had been seen, but only the presence of a mysterious something which had brushed past her in the dusk and vanished. Neither could Betsy Tucker's revelation, that she had heard footsteps in the corridor outside her bedroom on the night of the storm, and had seen the handle of her door turned, and the fright to the girl in consequence, be entirely ignored: for after it came to Miss Winter's ears, she had made inquiries of her servants, and could not learn that any one of them had been in the corridor that night. They had all been too much terrified by the storm, they declared, to quit their beds. Ella did not, would not, think much of this incident. The old house was full of strange noises, especially in stormy weather, and she herself, by giving way to her fancies, could readily have got into the way of believing that she heard footfalls and whispers and rustlings, for which she could not account, almost every night of her life.

But the strange assertion made by Maria Kettle was a very different matter; Ella could not help attaching more weight to it than to all that had gone before: and the extraordinary belief of poor Susan Keen, that her sister was alive and in the house, occurred unpleasantly to her mind. Could it be? Could it by any possibility be true that Katherine Keen was still alive, that she was hiding somewhere in the old Hall, and came out into the dark corridors on occasion to frighten people? Was it in very truth she herself, and not her spirit, that had been seen at different times? Ella's heart ached as it had never ached before. No, not even when the girl disappeared and could nowhere be found; though from that day life had never been quite the same to her. The dreadful uncertainty as to what had become of Katherine had added tenfold to the pain of losing her, and now, after the lapse of so long a time, it seemed as if the uncertainty would never be cleared up. But what if she had been alive all this time; alive, and close by? What if she had never quitted the roof of the Hall? Ella Winter's good sense urged her to reject such a theory as utterly untenable, certain difficulties presenting themselves palpably before her; but it urged her equally to reject that other theory of supernatural visitations. Between the two she knew not what to think. That Katherine had really been seen the evidence seemed conclusive. But had she been seen in the flesh, or in the spirit?

When a problem is put before you, which you find it impossible to solve, however anxious to do so, it is sometimes wise to lay it by for a while and turn the attention to other things, trusting to "the unforeseen" to do for you what you cannot do for yourself. Thus did Ella Winter in the present case. She was puzzled and distressed; and was growing a little bit nervous besides. Appetite failed; the long dark nights oppressed her, sleep gave place to wakeful restlessness, and she began to be afraid of sleeping alone. Therefore it was with a sigh of relief that she answered Mrs. Carlyon's invitation: and for the first time in her life she was not sorry to lose sight of the chimneys of Heron Dyke as the carriage whirled her and Maria Kettle away to the station.

Mrs. Carlyon had a surprise in store for her niece, as Ella discovered on the second evening after her arrival in London. Knowing her aunt's fondness for company, but being herself in no humour to enjoy it, Ella had pleaded for no large parties during her stay; that they should dine quietly *en famille*, and spend rational evenings. To this Mrs. Carlyon had readily agreed, stipulating, however, that the rule should be relaxed in favour of two or three people who might be called friends of the family.

"In short, my dear," Mrs. Carlyon had said, when talking of it the day of Ella's arrival, "I promise not to introduce you to a single stranger except one."

"Except one!" repeated Ella.

"Yes, except one. A very nice old gentleman who is between sixty and seventy years old. You won't surely object to *him!*"

Ella laughed. She thought she must not hold out against any gentleman of that age, but rather welcome his acquaintance.

But Miss Winter was very considerably taken aback when, on the following evening, her aunt led her up to a little, lean, finical-looking old man, who wore the attire of a bygone age, a brown wig, a long bottle-green coat, and curiously fine-frilled cambric linen, and introduced him: "Mr. Gilbert Denison of Nunham Priors."

For a moment or two Ella could find no word to say. She had unconsciously pictured Mr. Denison as a very truculent sort of individual; as what her uncle would have been with all the more disagreeable points of his character intensified; as a man who employed spies, and who would shrink from nothing in his endeavours to do his kinsman harm. Yet here before her she saw a very harmless-looking old gentleman indeed, with a puckered-up, comical, yet honest and kindly face, and dark, vivacious eyes that seemed brimming over with amusement at her evident discomfiture.

Mr. Denison took her hand with an old-world air of gallantry, and touched it with his lips.

"Enter the First Robber," he said, with one of his whimsical smiles. "I hope my ferocious appearance does not frighten you, young lady. You will get used to me better by-and-by, my dear. Why do you look so surprised? I cannot tell you how pleased I am to meet you."

He made room for her on the sofa by his side.

"Say now, I am not the sort of looking person you expected to find."

Ella smiled charmingly. Somehow she had taken a great and sudden fancy to him.

"I had always thought of you as being so different," she said.

"As an ogre, no doubt," he rejoined, with a comical nod. "I know. Poor Gilbert! he had his curious fancies, and one of them was to abuse me: I'm as sure of that as if I'd heard him. My dear, I cannot tell you how pleased I am to meet you. Confess now, that you had expected to see some dangerous kind of fellow in me: one that bites, eh?"

"No, indeed," returned Ella. "I am surprised because I had no expectation of seeing you."

"And you find me a worse hobgoblin than you imagined?"

"I do not find you one at all," she said, taking the place beside him.

"Well, well; a certain personage is said not to be so black as he is painted; let us hope that it will prove so in the present case. Ah! what a pity it is that Frank's not here to-night!" he added, abruptly.

"Your son, Mr. Denison?" asked Ella, her serious dark-blue eyes bent full upon him.

"Yes, my son; my will-o'-the-wisp, my ne'er-do-weel, the plague of my life," answered Mr. Denison. In his short, sharp sentences, and abrupt turns, Ella was put strongly in mind of her uncle.

"I should have been greatly pleased to meet him," she said. "Is he away from home?"

"Away from home!" exploded the old gentleman. "He's nearly always away from home. I never know to a thousand miles where to lay my finger on him. He might be a gipsy for restlessness. He is always gadding about from Dan to Beersheba. An incorrigible young fellow--a rolling stone that will never rest anywhere. I wish to goodness he would get married to some woman who knew how to tame him and make him settle down at home!"

Ella felt amused; her face showed it. Mr. Denison shook his head and frowned.

"Now, why couldn't Frank have married you, for instance?" he suddenly asked, after a brief pause.

This amused her more. "Dear Mr. Denison, I fear it would be altogether beyond my powers to tame so inveterate a roamer," she quietly said.

"Not at all--not at all. You are just the sort of woman to do it."

It seemed rather doubtful to Ella whether this ought to be taken as a compliment.

"It would have been so satisfactory, you know, to have had all the property in a nutshell--yours and mine," added the old gentleman. "Not that Frank need covet money: I shall be able to leave him some. But Heron Dyke ought to have been his--after me; he is nearer to it than you are. My dear, you have too much good sense, as I can see, to take offence at an old man's crotchets, and I am speaking to you as friend speaks to friend."

"I hope you will always so speak to me," warmly interrupted Ella.

"So I wish Frank could have known you--and taken a fancy to you, my dear. But I fear it is too late in the day to hope for anything so desirable. Frank never was particularly wise, and I have a sort of suspicion that what he would call his affections are engaged elsewhere: have thought it for some little time."

"Then I'm sure there can be no chance for me," cried Ella, merrily.

"Well, well; anything's better than his bringing over a black woman for a wife, and that's what I used to be afraid of at one time," continued Mr. Denison, nodding his head and his brown wig.

"I hope Frank will find his way back home in spring," he resumed, after a pause. "If you are in town about that time, Mrs. Carlyon and I must contrive to bring the pair of you together. There may be a chance yet. I don't suppose the young dog has forgotten how to make himself agreeable to the ladies, and he is considered not at all ill-looking--very much like what I was when younger."

This tried Ella's gravity a little. "As I think I said before, I shall be pleased to make your son's acquaintance," she said, demurely.

"But whether Frank comes home or not, my dear, I must have you down at Nunham in spring. You will find many things there that you have never seen before and will have little opportunity of seeing elsewhere. You are intelligent as well as sensible, and I feel sure that you will be interested."

Next to picking up a bargain in the auction-rooms, nothing delighted Mr. Denison more than to secure an appreciative listener while he descanted on the rarity and value of some of his favourite curiosities; and this he found in Ella. Ella on her part was very glad to have met him. He was a man to esteem and like, despite his eccentricities: and she felt thankful to know that the breach in the family, which had existed so many years, was healed at last. Her face flushed as she recollected that if the fear, tormenting her latterly, had grounds, Heron Dyke was not hers, but Mr. Denison's.

She did not see him again during her stay in London, for he went away to Nunham Priors. Ella was by no means certain, had he remained, that she should not have imparted to him all her doubts and fears. He and she were alike honest, wishing always to act rightly.

Her own stay in London only extended to a week: she did not like to spare more time from home at present. The week passed pleasantly and quickly;

and both she and Maria Kettle returned to the Hall in better health and spirits than they were in when they quitted it.

Gossip in remote hamlets and small country towns, more especially if the subject of it be some well-known personage, grows and spreads with a rapidity unknown to the rankest tropical weed, and Nullington was no exception to the rule. It had now become matter of common talk in the town, that there was something mysterious and unexplained with regard to Squire Denison's death. How or whence such an idea originated, or what the mysterious something might be, people did not care to ask; and if they did there was nobody to answer. Facts that are only half known, or that are wildly guessed at, have always more fascination for ordinary minds than uncompromising truths that stand boldly out in the light of day, and which anyone can examine for themselves.

The Nullingtonians seized on the rumour with avidity, and one may be sure that it suffered nothing from loss or diminution in its transit from mouth to mouth. It was not long in reaching the ears of Nixon, the agent whom Mr. Plackett had formerly employed to report to him respecting the state of Mr. Denison's health, and the general progress of matters at the Hall. Nixon had been away from Nullington for a time, possibly prosecuting inquiries elsewhere, and these rumours greeted him on his return. Putting aside any pecuniary benefit he might gain, Nixon was naturally a man of prying and inquisitive disposition; nothing pleased him better than worming out the secrets of other people. He went about the town asking guarded questions of this person and the other, trying to put the various fragments of gossip together and trace them to their fountain-head. Altogether, he contrived to make out something like a coherent whole: upon which he favoured the London firm, Messrs. Plackett, Plackett and Rex, with a long and confidential letter.

The letter brought down Mr. Charles Plackett, Nixon meeting him by appointment at the railway station. The two had some private conversation together.

"What we cannot understand in your report is this one item," observed Mr. Charles Plackett: "that Miss Winter herself suspects some fraud has been at work, and is as anxious to have matters investigated as we could be."

"I assure you, sir, I believe it to be so," affirmed Nixon. "My information on this point came from a sure source."

"Well, I intend to go to see her," said Mr. Charles Plackett.

Nixon opened his eyes.

"To go to see her, sir! What, at Heron Dyke?"

"Yes. Why not? It is the only step I can take: and, whether it brings forth fruit or not, I shall at any rate see how the land lies with regard to herself. If she is, as you think, anxious for the investigation, she is a good and honourable young lady; that's all I can say."

Mr. Charles Plackett took a fly and drove over to Heron Dyke. He sent in his card to Miss Winter, and was at once admitted. Ella was alone. Maria Kettle had returned to the Vicarage, and Mrs. Toynbee was not yet back from London. Ella knew that the Placketts were Mr. Denison's solicitors, and she supposed this gentleman had come to bring her some message from him. That idea, however, was at once dispelled.

"I am come here this morning, Miss Winter, upon rather a curious errand," began Mr. Plackett in his cheerful, chirruping way. "But before going any farther, it may be as well to say that I am come without the knowledge of my esteemed client, Mr. Denison, of Nunham Priors. In fact I am adopting a most unusual course with a lawyer; I am venturing to intrude upon you entirely on my own account."

Miss Winter bowed. "I shall be pleased to hear anything that you may have to communicate," she said frankly.

Mr. Plackett paused. "I am somewhat non-plussed in what way to begin," he confessed, with a smile.

"A difficulty, I should imagine, that does not often arise with gentlemen of your profession," observed Ella, courteously.

The little lawyer laughed. "I believe you are not far wrong there, Miss Winter. Perhaps my best plan will be to plunge at once *in medias res*. I may say, then, that some disquieting rumours have reached our ears--and when I say 'ours,' in this instance I mean my own--having reference to certain events which took place in this house during your absence abroad. The events I allude to are the illness and death of the late Mr. Denison. What we have heard would almost lead us to imagine that deception of some kind, if not fraud itself, was at work in the case; and--and----"

He paused. Ella waited.

"Frankly speaking, Miss Winter, I have heard a report that these rumours have reached yourself; and I am here to ask you--but pray do not answer the question unless you feel fully at liberty to do so--whether that is a fact?"

"Yes, it is," she freely answered. "I have heard the rumours."

"Ah! Just so. Thank you very much for your frankness. I presume, however, that you attach very little importance to them?"

"On the contrary, I attach very considerable importance to them. I do not say they are true--far from it; on the other hand, I do not know but they may be. The doubt renders me very uneasy."

"Really now! I'm sure there are not many young ladies like you, for truth and candour. But--pardon my presumption--may I ask whether you have been able to trace the rumours to any foundation? Perhaps you have not tried to do so?"

"I have tried," replied Ella. "I have used every effort to track them back to their source, though it is not much, of course, that it lies in my power to do."

"And the result,--if I may dare to ask it?"

"There is no result. None. I cannot discover whether they are worthy of belief, or whether they are fabrications. That certain unnecessary precautions were observed during my late uncle's illness--green baize doors put up to shield him from the household; friends never admitted to him; a mysterious kind of professional nurse had down from London to attend him--is true. But those about him, Dr. Jago and old Aaron Stone, explain all this away with perfect plausibility."

Charles Plackett mused. "No, of course not; there was not much you could do," he remarked, apparently speaking to himself.

"An individual, whom I will not name, warned me that Heron Dyke was not legally mine," resumed Miss Winter. "I was startled, as you may suppose; but I could elicit nothing further. Nothing but what I tell you--that I held Heron Dyke by fraud."

"Dear me!"

"I did not know whether to believe it, or not; I do not know now. I carried the tale to Mr. Daventry, and I spoke also to my uncle's old friend, the Vicar of Nullington. Neither of them attached the smallest credibility to the charge; they almost ridiculed it. Mr. Daventry says that nothing whatever could deprive me of Heron Dyke, save my uncle's not having lived to see his seventieth birthday. And several persons saw him and conversed with him subsequently to that date."

"I did, for one," remarked Mr. Charles Plackett. "Well, I don't see that there's much to be done. You say you will not give up the name of the individual who----"

"No," she interrupted. "And if I did give it, the end would not be answered. He--he--is no longer here; he could not be questioned."

"It is one of the most puzzling questions I ever had to do with, madam. Heron Dyke is a fine property. You would not like to give it up."

"I would give it up to-day if I were sure it were Mr. Denison's. I wish I was sure--one way or the other. If it is not mine it must be his, and he would have every right to it. Does he know of this doubt?"

"Not a word."

"I met him a short while ago, when I was in London. He came to my aunt's, Mrs. Carlyon. I took a great fancy to him."

Mr. Charles Plackett smiled. "And he took a fancy to a certain young lady--if I may say as much. He called at our office the next day, before returning to Nunham Priors. What do you think he said, Miss Winter?--that he did not so much regret the loss of Heron Dyke now, when he saw what charming hands held it."

Ella rather shrank from the compliment. "I and my interests are as nothing, Mr. Plackett, in comparison with arriving at the truth. If fraud and deception have been at work, it is to the advantage of everyone that they should be exposed and frustrated."

Mr. Plackett gazed on her glowing face admiringly. "If everyone thought and acted like you, my dear young lady," he said, "I am afraid that the occupation of us poor lawyers would soon become a thing of the past."

"That would be a catastrophe indeed," responded Ella, with a laugh.

A little more conversation ensued. One word leading to another, Ella confided to him what the servant Eliza had told her--that she had penetrated beyond the green baize doors, on one lucky occasion when they were left unguarded, and had found the Squire's rooms empty: Mr. Denison was nowhere to be seen in them. Nay, more; the rooms and the bed appeared to be unoccupied.

Mr. Plackett, though evidently much surprised, could still make nothing of it. He sat fingering his grey hair--a habit of his when in thought. Ella finished by inquiring what more she could do.

"I really fail to see at present that there is anything more you can do," he answered. "And I am quite sure that not one person in a thousand would do as much as you have already done."

"Are you sure it was my uncle you saw," she inquired, speaking on the moment's impulse, "when you were here two days after his birthday?"

Mr. Charles Plackett paused, revolving the question. "I thought I was sure," he said. "Although I had only seen Mr. Denison twice before, and that some years previously, he certainly seemed to me to be the same individual, naturally much wasted and changed by illness. One thing I perfectly remembered: the beautiful cat's-eye ring he wore. Yes, I think it could have been no other than Mr. Denison--and no other temper than his. You heard, probably, of the passion he went into?"

"And threw away his beef-tea, and broke the cup. Truly I cannot imagine anyone doing that, save my uncle."

"I must say that I have not been so thoroughly puzzled by any case for a long while," remarked the lawyer, as he rose to depart.

And puzzled Mr. Plackett was destined to remain; at least for some time yet to come. If Miss Winter had looked to benefit by his advice, she was disappointed. He had no advice of any consequence to offer. He could only thank her again for her frankness, and say that he would consult with his client, Mr. Denison, and, with her permission, write to her in the course of a few days. Then, declining refreshments, he left the Hall, much more disquieted in his mind than when he had arrived at it.

But within an hour of the lawyer's departure, Miss Winter had something else to think about than his promise to write to her. There came a telegram from Edward Conroy. He had reached London, and hoped to be at Heron Dyke on the morrow.

CHAPTER V.

A FRUITLESS ERRAND

Matters with Philip Cleeve were not progressing quite to his satisfaction. Upon going down to breakfast one morning, he was surprised to find his mother down before him. A notable thing; for Lady Cleeve was seldom able to rise early. Philip kissed her fondly.

"This is a rare treat, mother," he said. "It seems like old times come back again."

She pressed his hand and smiled tenderly in his bright, handsome face. "I want to have a little talk with you before you go out, Philip. I sat up for you last night, but you came home late."

"Ah, yes, to be sure," replied Philip hurriedly, very conscious that he was too often late. "I went round to George Winstone's lodgings, and the time slipped away."

"So long as you were enjoying yourself, dear, it was quite right," answered Lady Cleeve. In her eyes Philip could do no wrong.

"And what is it, mother, that you have to say to me?" he asked, carelessly taking up a piece of toast and playing with the butter-knife. He was growing vaguely uneasy already.

"I met Mr. Tiplady yesterday," began Lady Cleeve: and Philip put down the knife without using it. His heart sank within him. "I had to call in at Wharton's about my broken spectacles, and there I found Mr. Tiplady having a new key fitted to his watch. We came away together, and I took the opportunity of reminding him of his promise, given so long ago, to take you into partnership. He had by no means forgotten it, he said, and was willing that the question should be brought to a practical issue as soon as I pleased. Of course you will not take a full share at present: he intimated that: only a small one. But it will be a very great thing for you, Philip; and you can afford to wait."

Philip made no comment upon this. Lady Cleeve continued.

"I thanked him for his generosity. It *is* generous of him," she added, "to admit you with only a poor thousand pounds----"

"He does not want money," interrupted Philip, resentfully. "Tiplady is as rich as can be--and he has nobody to come after him."

"He is none the less generous; many men in his position would not take in a partner under several thousands of pounds," returned Lady Cleeve. "What I wanted to tell you was this, dear--that he will probably speak to you to-day. There need not be any further delay. Mr. Daventry will draw up the deed of partnership, and nothing will then remain but for you to pay over the money."

Philip rose abruptly and pushed back his chair. Then he turned and gazed through the window to hide his emotion. "You have not done breakfast, dear," cried Lady Cleeve in dismay. "You have eaten scarcely anything."

"I have done very well indeed, thank you, mother," he answered from the window. "I have one of my headaches this morning."

"Poor boy! the news is a delightful surprise to him," thought Lady Cleeve. "Philip is just as sensitive as he used to be."

Philip got away from his mother and the house as quickly as possible, walking along the road like a man in a dream. The thousand pounds, or the greater portion of what was left of it, had gone out of his hands to Captain Lennox. Or, rather, to that blessed company that the Captain was just now so eager over. Early though it was, Philip must see him; and he bent his steps towards The Lilacs.

As he went along, the thought struck him that he had not seen Lennox about very lately. The last time Philip called, he was told by the man-servant that the Captain had gone out for the day, and Mrs. Ducie was ill with a cold.

It was a servant-maid who answered Philip's nervous ring at the house this morning. Her master was in London, she said.

"In London!" exclaimed Philip. "When did he go?"

"Rather more than a week ago, I think, sir," was the girl's answer.

"I want to see Captain Lennox particularly," rejoined Philip.

"I dare say he will be back soon now, sir. I've not heard that he means to make a long stay this time."

Philip pondered.

"Can I see Mrs. Ducie? Ask her to pardon the early hour and see me for a minute--if she will be so kind."

"Mrs. Ducie can't see you now, sir," dissented the maid; "she is not yet up. Her cold keeps very bad, and she hardly comes down at all."

"Can you take a message to her?"

"Oh yes, sir, I can do that. Her breakfast is just gone up."

"Give my kind regards to Mrs. Ducie, and ask her if she will tell me when the Captain will be at home."

The maid ran upstairs and soon came down with the return message. Mrs. Ducie's very kind regards to Mr. Cleeve, and she had not the least notion when. Not for a few days, she thought: as his last letter, received yesterday, said nothing about it.

Philip turned away from The Lilacs as wise as he had gone, hardly heeding which way he took, save that it was from the office instead of to it. Knowing what he knew, he asked himself how it was possible for him to face Tiplady's inquiries? Out of the twelve hundred pounds given him by his mother so short a time ago, to be held by him as a sacred trust, only a balance of eighty-five pounds remained in the bank.

It is true that if Captain Lennox's prognostications respecting the splendid future of the Hermandad Silver Mining Company should prove to be correct, Philip Cleeve would more than recoup himself in the whole sum which he was now deficient. When Lennox first bought the shares for him, he had assured Philip that no further calls would be made: but despite this assurance two heavy calls had since had to be met, for "expenses;" calls which had gone far towards exhausting Philip's remaining resources. Captain Lennox had made no secret of his own disappointment and annoyance, but he was as sanguine as ever of ultimate success, and he had put it so strongly to Philip whether it would not be wiser to double his venture, rather than forfeit the sum already invested, that the latter had agreed to meet the calls, although not without a sadly misgiving heart.

As matters, however, had now turned out, he must find Lennox at once and show him the necessity for the shares being disposed of without delay. In that, Philip anticipated no difficulty, as the shares were so much sought after. Or else he must get Captain Lennox to go with him to Lady Cleeve and Mr. Tiplady, and explain to them how well the money was invested, and persuade them that in view of the splendid profits sure to accrue before long, it would be folly to sell out just now. Evidently the first thing to be done was to find Captain Lennox.

A little comforted in mind by the fact of having arrived at some sort of a decision, he made his way with hesitating steps to the office. It was a relief to him to find that Mr. Tiplady had started by an early train for Norwich, and would not be back till night. This gave Philip breathing-time, for which he was thankful.

Getting his dinner away, he spent the evening with some friends; and was careful not to reach home until sure his mother would be in bed. That night, on his sleepless pillow, he decided on his plans.

Early in the morning, before Lady Cleeve could be downstairs, Philip snatched a hasty breakfast and went out. He left a note for his mother, in which he told her that he had to go suddenly to London on business, and she was not to be surprised or alarmed if he did not return till the evening of the following day. Then he despatched a nearly identical note to Mr. Tiplady, which Philip thought a clever hit. Lady Cleeve would take it that he was away on business connected with the office; while Mr. Tiplady would be sure to imagine that it was on some affairs of his mother he was despatched to London. Making his way to the railway-station, Philip caught a passing train, and was whirled away to the metropolis.

When in London, Captain Lennox generally stayed at his favourite hotel, the Piazza, in Covent Garden; this Philip knew, and he drove there direct from the station. The urbane individual who was fetched to answer his inquiries, and who had more the look of a church dignitary than of a head waiter, told Philip that, although Captain Lennox was, as he surmised, frequently at the hotel, he had not been there lately. For the past six weeks, or so, they had not seen him, neither were they in a position to afford any information as to his whereabouts. All that Philip could do was to dissemble his disappointment and go.

This seemed to Philip a worse check than the one at The Lilacs the previous morning. Halting in the street, he bethought himself what he could do--where look for Lennox. Only one place presented itself to his mind: and that was the office of the Hermandad Company. It was situate in the City, New Broad Street. If he did not see the Captain there, he should at least hear where he was to be found. But Philip thought he most likely should see him.

Half an hour's drive in a hansom cab took him to Broad Street; and to the proper number, at which the cabman readily drew up. But Philip could not so easily find the office he was in search of. On a large board outside the doorway were painted up the names of some thirty or forty different firms or companies, each of them occupying offices in the same building. Philip at length discovered the name he wanted, the last but two on the list, and was directed to mount to the third floor.

On the third floor--and a very dingy, unwholesome-smelling floor it was, for the building was an old one--he found the Hermandad office. Philip's imagination had led him to fancy the offices of so important a company as rather grand and imposing: this did not look like it. The door was shut, and he could not open it. He knocked again and again, but without response. While wondering at all this, and standing to think what he could do next, an opposite door was opened, and a sharp-looking youth came out.

"Nobody at home here apparently," remarked Philip, pointing to the door. "What's the best time to find them in?"

"Don't know," answered the youth, twisting his mouth into a grin. "Nobody been here for a fortnight, but a boy to fetch letters."

"Nobody been here for a fortnight!" exclaimed Philip.

"Nobody else. Not likely. Silver-mining company, hey! Oh, Jemima!"

Philip could have wrung the boy's neck.

"Are you one of the green 'uns?" continued he. "Lots of 'em come. No use, though; not a bit; only have to go away again. Fishy--awful! Next akin to smashing up."

With these strange remarks, the boy shot off, sliding down the banisters; leaving Philip feeling sick at heart.

The Hermandad mine had evidently failed, and its company come to grief. A suspicion stole over Philip that Captain Lennox might be more hardly hit than the world suspected, and was keeping out of the way.

What to do, he knew not. Was there anything that he could do next, except go back home and reveal everything to his mother? He had tasted nothing all day, save his morsel of breakfast; and, although he had no appetite, he felt so faint that he knew he must take refreshment of some kind if he did not wish his strength to break down. Turning into the nearest restaurant, he called for a glass of wine, and tried to study the carte; but the names of the different dishes conveyed no definite ideas to his mind.

"Bring me anything you have ready." he said wearily to the waiter; "a basin of soup will do." And then he lay back in his chair and shut his eyes.

The waiter had just put some soup before him, and was about to take off the cover, when Philip started to his feet with an exclamation. "By heavens! I never thought of that!" Staring around, he sat down in a little confusion: for the moment he had forgotten where he was. The waiter looked askance at him, to discover whether he was mad.

But the fact was that Philip had had what seemed to him nothing less than a flash of inspiration. He had suddenly remembered that there was such a person as Freddy Bootle in existence. Why not go to him in his trouble? Freddy was rich, and as kindhearted as he was rich; he was not the sort of man to allow a friend to sink for want of a helping hand: in any case Philip felt sure of his sympathy and advice. Eating his soup with some degree of relish, he paid, and drove off in a hansom to Mr. Bootle's rooms in Bond Street.

Philip felt desperate. Especially at the thought of having to reveal his folly to his mother, and her consequent distress. That seemed worse than the loss of the money itself. Never had his conduct, his almost criminal weakness, presented itself to him in so odious a light as now. Had the money been absolutely his own, had it been bequeathed to him by will or come to him by any mode other than that by which it had come, he could have borne to lose it with comparative equanimity. But when he called to mind the fact that the sum which it had taken him so short a time to dissipate was the accumulation of long years of patient pinching and hoarding on the part of his mother, that it represented many a self-denied luxury, many a harmless pleasure ruthlessly sacrificed, and that all this had been done to ensure the advancement in life of his worthless self, he was almost ready to think that the sooner the world were rid of him the better for everyone concerned. How could he ever bear to face again that mother and her thoughtful love?--how witness her pained face when he should declare his folly? *Must* she be told? If only Freddy Bootle would give him a help in this strait, what a different man he would be in time to come!

It was a break in the bitterness of his thoughts when the cab drew up at Mr. Bootle's lodgings. Philip was not kept long in suspense. An elderly man answered his knock and ring. The elderly man was sorry to say that Mr. Bootle was in Rome at present, and was not expected back till after Christmas.

"Was there ever so unlucky a wretch as I?" murmured Philip to himself, as he turned, more sick at heart than ever, from the door. His one and only hope had failed him.

The short winter day was drawing to a close, and the lamps were being lighted as he turned into Piccadilly. He wandered about aimlessly for some time, into this street and that, stopping now and again to stare into a shop-window, or at the unending procession of vehicles in the busier streets, and then wandering on again without seeming to see anything.

All at once he was startled into the most vivid life. Coming towards him, but yet a little distance away, and with several of the hurrying crowd between them, he saw Captain Lennox. The light from a shop-window shone full on his pale, strongly-marked features, and there could be no mistake. Philip sprang forward eagerly, and the sudden movement seemed to have the effect of attracting the Captain's glance towards him. For one brief moment there came, or Philip thought there did, a gleam of recognition into those steel-blue eyes; the next, they and their owner were alike hidden by the intervening crowd.

Philip Cleeve shouldered his way along more roughly than he had ever done before; in a few seconds he was standing on the exact spot where he had seen Lennox, but that individual was no longer visible. He had vanished as completely as if the earth had swallowed him up. Philip stared about him, like a man suddenly moonstruck, unheedful of the jostling and elbowing of the passersby. Up the street and down the street he gazed, but no Captain Lennox was to be seen. What *could* have become of him?

"Surely he need not hide himself from me!" thought Philip. "We are both in the same boat."

Looking about for the Captain, in a sort of amazed doubt, Philip saw that he stood close before the open door of a large drapery emporium, Was it possible that Lennox had taken refuge inside? No sooner did the thought flash across Philip's mind, than he marched boldly into the shop. There were several people there, customers and assistants, but no signs of the man he was seeking. A civil assistant came up to ask what they could serve him with, and Philip frankly avowed the cause of his entering. A friend--a gentleman-- had suddenly disappeared before he could reach him; he could only think he had entered the shop.

"Very possibly," the young man replied; and as he was not to be seen in it now, he might have passed through it, and left by the opposite door.

Then Philip saw that the shop was what might be called a double one; that is to stay, that it had a door and window opening into another street. Had Lennox walked in at one door and out at the other, without stopping to purchase anything? It was the conclusion Philip came to. He recognised the uselessness of further pursuit of Lennox. It was clear that the Captain had purposely evaded meeting him: the reason for such evasion was not far to seek. Philip purchased a pair of gloves, and then pursued his aimless way, weary and downcast.

Where should he go, and what should he do? He knew not, and he did not greatly care. He was there alone in the huge wilderness of London, without one living creature that knew him or that cared for him. It was not too late to take the last train home; but he had a fixed repugnance against doing so. Why hasten to meet his mother's reproachful eyes, and Mr. Tiplady's incisive questionings? And yet, if he stayed the night in London, he must face those ordeals on the morrow. What could the morrow bring him, more than to-day had brought? Still he wandered aimlessly on, through one mile of street after another, his thoughts brimming over with bitterness at the recollection of all his mad folly. What now to him but mad folly seemed those nights at The Lilacs when, flushed with wine, he had staked his mother's savings on the turn of a card, and had seen the gold, hoarded by her for his sake, swept almost contemptuously into the pockets of such men as Camberley and Lennox, who, the moment his back was turned, probably sneered at him as a jay parading in peacock's plumes? What now to him, but folly, seemed the spells which he had allowed to be woven round him by the witcheries of Margaret Ducie? In his heart of hearts he had never really cared for her, however much at the time he might fancy that he had--not even when her hold over him had seemed the strongest. And now, when he looked back, she assumed in his thoughts the semblance of one of those specious phantoms, lovely to look upon, but who seem sent only to lure weak-minded fools to destruction.

Poor Philip! From the burning thoughts within him rose next another phantom. Nothing specious about *her*, but pure and saint-like as a lily steeped in dew--the image of Maria Kettle. Had he indeed lost her? He knew now how much she was to him; that he had never loved but her.

Yes, she was surely lost to him for ever. He would have no home to take her to, and no prospect of winning a position for himself: a life of commonplace drudgery, of separation from the only woman he had ever loved, or could love, was all that now lay before him.

Still onward, ever onward, went he in his pain.

"Oh, my darling, you might have saved me if you would!" he cried. "You might, you might!"

Still onward, ever onward. From tower and steeple the hours were clanged out one after another, but he heeded them not. It was close upon midnight when he found himself standing on one of the great bridges that span the Thames. Far away into the blackness on either side of him the great city spread itself out, seeming to his imagination, at that hour, like some huge monster that was slowly settling itself down to sleep. Silently below him ran the sullen river, stealthily carrying its dread secrets down to the sea. Here and there a few feeble lamps mocked the darkness.

Philip Cleeve stood and gazed over the parapet into the black-flowing stream below. How many unhappy men might not have flung off life's bitter burden at that very spot! How easy the process! A leap, a plunge, a minute's brief struggle, and then the deep, deep sleep that knows no waking. Could it be really wrong to throw away that which was no longer of any value, that which had become a burden and for which he no longer cared? The question kept coming back to him with a sort of dreadful fascination. He could hear the faint lapping of the tide against the piers; and, the longer he gazed down at the water, the more it seemed to whisper to him of peace and rest, and a quiet ending to all his troubles. Why not quit a world in which there no longer seemed a place for him? Why not?

Suddenly there arose a sound behind him, as of the quick patter of feet. Before Philip had time to interfere, before he well knew what had happened, a female figure, scantily clad, and with hair flying to the winds, had sprung on one of the stone seats, and thence on to the parapet. For one brief instant she stood thus, dimly outlined against the starlit sky; then, with hands clasped above her head, and a low, wild cry, she sprang headlong to her death.

A little crowd gathered, as if by magic, where there had seemed to be scarcely anyone a minute before. Faint at heart, dizzy with the sudden horror of the thing, Philip Cleeve fell back from the rest. What were his little troubles compared with those which must have driven that poor desperate creature to destruction? The black, sullen river had suddenly become hateful to him, and he made haste to leave it far behind.

CHAPTER VI.

COUNSEL TAKEN WITH MR. MEATH

Anxious revelations were those which Ella Winter had to pour into the ears of her lover! For he was by her side now, not to leave her for long together again. The cloud, which during the last few months had been lowering over her life, was lightened at last; the burdens which had been growing too heavy for her to bear, were lifted now upon shoulders stronger and more able to sustain them. Suspense and distress lay around her still; but, compared with what had been, she walked in sunshine, gladness in her eyes and in her heart, and Love's sweet whispers in her ears.

Edward Conroy took up his quarters at the hotel in Nullington, whence he walked over frequently to Heron Dyke. Mrs. Toynbee, back at the Hall now, was not slow to perceive the state of affairs. She wrote to her friend and patroness, Lady Dimsdale, that she was afraid she should have to look out for another home before long: for, unless she was much mistaken, Miss Winter was about to marry. The gentleman, she was good enough to say, was a very pleasant, nice-mannered person, named Conroy; but it seemed to her a great pity that Miss Winter had not chosen someone more nearly her equal in the social scale.

The weather was mild and open for the time of year, and Conroy and Ella were much out of doors. During these rambles, the conversation often turned upon past affairs--and many a consultation took place as to what could be done to bring to light all that still remained doubtful and obscure.

There was so much of it--taken as a whole. So many points that presented their own difficulties. The doubt as to whether Ella was the legal inheritor of Heron Dyke; the disappearance of Katherine Keen, and the superstition that arose out of it; the murder of the ill-fated Hubert Stone, and the robbery of the jewels: all these were matters of grave perplexity, upon which no light had yet been thrown.

Edward Conroy was puzzled by it all--just as Mr. Charles Plackett had been. He seemed never to tire of questioning Ella on this point and on that, and made notes sometimes of her answers: but he was none the nearer seeing his way to any elucidation.

"Have you fully calculated what the result to yourself will be if it is discovered that fraud has been at work?" he said to her one day, when they had been speaking of what had happened at Heron Dyke during her absence.

"Fully," replied Ella.

"Home, money, and lands--all will go from you."

"I know it. But would you have had me act otherwise than as I have acted?--would you have had me keep the doubt to myself?"

"Not for worlds."

"I think--I think, Edward, you are as anxious to discover the truth as I am."

"Quite as anxious."

"Although it be against your own interest. After all, it may be that you will have a penniless wife, compared with the rich one you expected."

"So much the better. She will owe all the more to me, and the world cannot then say that I have married her for her fortune."

"As if you cared for anything the world might choose to say!"--and to this remark Mr. Conroy slightly laughed in answer.

He had not been more than a day or two at Heron Dyke, when Miss Winter put into his hands the malachite and gold sleeve-link which Betsy Tucker had sent her by Mrs. Keen. Betsy was recovering slowly from her illness; all danger was over.

"I should like to see the young woman, and question her," observed he, turning the link about in his hand, as he examined it critically.

"There will be no difficulty," said Ella. "Betsy has been out for one airing, and she can come here. Why do you look at the trinket so attentively? Have you ever seen it before?"

"Never. But it is one of rather remarkable workmanship."

A fly brought Betsy Tucker to the Hall. There, in the presence of Mr. Conroy, she was requested to point out the place, as nearly as she could recollect it, where she had picked up the link. It was within a few yards of the spot where Hubert Stone was found. The girl had nothing more to tell, and sobbed out her contrition for her fault. Miss Winter was everything that was kind; but Mr. Conroy, speaking sternly, warned her not to disclose a word to anyone about the affair or there was no telling what the consequences to herself might be. The girl, with many tears, promised faithfully to keep the secret, and seemed only too glad to be let off so easily.

The sleeve-link had not belonged, so far as could be ascertained, to Hubert: whether it had, or had not, been the property of his assailant, was another matter. If so, it must have been wrenched from his sleeve during the scuffle; and, as Edward Conroy shrewdly remarked, it proved that the assailant was a gentleman. No man in an inferior station would be likely to wear such a link.

"I shall run up to town to-morrow," said Edward Conroy to Ella, when the interview was over and they were alone.

"To town! For anything in particular?"

"Merely to put this malachite and gold trinket into certain hands," he added. "If this link can be traced out to its owner, it may lead to some discoveries."

Mr. Conroy accordingly went to London. This, it will be noted, was within two or three days of his first arrival at Heron Dyke. He returned from London the following day, having put matters, together with the sleeve-stud, as he informed Miss Winter, into efficient hands. Taking up his abode, as before, at Nullington, he passed a considerable portion of his time at Heron Dyke.

Months before this, Conroy had heard tell of the strange disappearance of Katherine Keen; but only now was he made aware that the Hall was supposed to be haunted by her presence. He listened to the story of how the two maids, whom Aaron Stone had afterwards discharged in consequence, had positively asserted that they saw her looking down upon them from the gallery; he heard the story of Mrs. Carlyon's fright, and of Maria Kettle's strange experience not long ago. The evidence, taken collectively, was too strong to be altogether ignored, despite his inclination so to treat it.

"I wish the ghost would favour me with a visit!" he heartily exclaimed. "I would do my best to put its unsubstantiality to the proof."

"I know not which would be the worse: to find that Katherine is in the Hall in the flesh--that she is not dead, as her poor sister believes--or that the house is haunted by her spirit," breathed Miss Winter in answer.

"Have you any objection to my exploring this north wing?" he inquired, after a pause of thought.

"Not the least. I should be thankful for you to do so."

Mr. Conroy lost no time. That same afternoon he ascended to the north wing; and did not come down until he had visited every nook and corner of it. Room after room, passage after passage, closet after closet, he examined, and satisfied himself that no person or thing was hidden in them. Taking the precaution to lock the doors, he brought the keys away with him.

"Troubled spirits never walk by daylight, I believe," remarked Mrs. Toynbee to him. She had never relished the superstitious tales. "We must look for them by dark, Mr. Conroy, if at all."

"That is just what I mean to do," replied Conroy.

And accordingly he took to rambling about the north wing in the dusk of evening, in the hope that, one time or another, he should encounter the supposed ghost. He would sit for half an hour at a time, silent and immovable, in the darkest corner of the gallery, with no company but the mice busy at work behind the wainscot. "I may have to wait for weeks," he said to Ella, "but if there be any ghost at all, I shall be sure to see it by-and-by."

One evening when dusk was creeping on, a certain Mr. Meath arrived at the Hall, a telegram to Conroy having given previous notice that he might be expected; and he was at once admitted.

The stranger was the chief of a well-known inquiry-office in London: it was to him that Conroy had confided the sleeve-link. He was a tall, lanky, angular-boned man of sixty, with dyed hair and a slow, deferential smile. He always dressed in black, as being the most becoming wear for a gentleman, and that he invariably looked the latter Mr. Meath was fully persuaded; whereas he had in fact more of the air of a prosperous undertaker than of anything else. In his peculiar profession he was known to be a shrewd and practised man.

He was shown into one of the smaller drawing-rooms. No sooner had Edward Conroy entered it and sat down, than Mr. Meath arose and satisfied himself that the door was really shut, and that no one was hidden behind the curtains.

"Excuse these little precautions, sir," he said with his deferential smile, "but I have more than once had occasion to prove the value of them."

"Oh, no doubt. Your telegram stated that you had some news for me, Mr. Meath," added Conroy.

"I have some news for you, sir--news which may prove of importance. Before proceeding any further in the matter, I thought it would be as well to let you know the result already arrived at, and take your instructions with regard to future proceedings."

Hitching his chair nearer the table, Mr. Meath drew forth a little box from one of his pockets. "Here is the sleeve-link," he said, as he opened the box. "You have doubtless observed, sir, that it is of rather a curious and uncommon pattern?"

"Yes. If you remember I said so when I saw you in town."

"On examining this under a powerful glass," continued Mr. Meath, "I presently detected what I felt nearly sure could be nothing less than the private mark of the firm that had manufactured it. I took the link to the foreman of a large firm of jewellers with whom I had had some transactions previously, and he at once confirmed my view. 'There could be no doubt it was the manufacturer's mark,' he said. The question was--who were the manufacturers?"

"He did not know."

"He did not know, sir. But he thought he might be able to find out, if I would leave the link with him for a couple of days. Which I agreed to."

"And did he?" asked Mr. Conroy.

The private-inquiry officer solemnly nodded.

"At the end of the couple of days he sent for me, sir, and told me he had discovered the private mark to be that of Messrs. Wooler and Wooler, of Piccadilly. An eminent firm--as perhaps you know, Mr. Conroy."

"I have heard the name."

"To Messrs. Wooler I accordingly went, disclosed as much of the affair to them as was necessary, and stated what I wanted to know. They were most obliging, and at once promised to consult their books. Yesterday they sent for me. They had found from their books that the sleeve-link I now hold in my hand was one of a pair which, together with various other articles of which they were good enough to furnish me with a list and description, had been supplied by them about four years ago to a certain Major Piper, then living at Cheltenham. May I ask you, sir, whether you happen to be acquainted with any such gentleman; or whether he is known in this neighbourhood?" concluded the speaker, after making a brief pause.

"I am not. And I cannot tell you whether he is known in the neighbourhood: I am nearly a stranger to it myself. But I can inquire of the ladies here," added Conroy, rising to quit the room.

He returned, saying that Miss Winter did not know anyone of the name. Mrs. Toynbee did. She had met a Major Piper once or twice in society, but not lately; and she believed him to be a highly respectable man. "I have the Major's address at Cheltenham in my pocket-book," said Meath; "or rather what was his address four years ago. It is quite possible that he may have gone away from the town, or have died in the interim."

"Very possible indeed," answered Conroy.

"It rests with you to decide whether you think it worth while to proceed any farther in the case. If this Major Piper be still at Cheltenham, there will not be any difficulty in finding him: if he is not, there may be, especially should it turn out that he is what we call a shady individual. Difficulty, and also expense."

"Having gone so far, I certainly think we ought to go farther," answered Conroy. "Are you not of that opinion yourself?"

"I am, sir: but, as I say, it is for you to decide. We have got hold of a clue of some sort. Whether it will lead us up to what we want to know, time and perseverance only can prove."

"I certainly think Major Piper ought to be found. As to expense, I gave you carte-blanche for that when I was in London."

"Then I will proceed in the matter without delay," said Mr. Meath, rising. "And I hope, sir, I shall shortly have something further to report to you."

"You will take something before you go away," said Conroy, ringing the bell.

Putting down the hat he had taken up, Mr. Meath acknowledged that he would be glad of something. A tray of refreshments was brought in; and presently he had departed as silently as he had come.

A few days elapsed, during a portion of which Edward Conroy was away upon his own affairs. Close upon his return, Mr. Meath again made his way to Heron Dyke, calling, as before, in the dusk of the evening. Miss Winter had grown anxious as to the result of the inquiries, and she told Edward Conroy that she should like to be present during the interview, if there were no objection.

There was no objection, Conroy said, and took her into the room with him. They all sat down together.

"I have been more successful than I ventured to anticipate," began Mr. Meath, in his slow way--which Edward Conroy somewhat impatiently interrupted.

"Then you have found Major Piper?"

"I have found Major Piper, sir: I had very little difficulty in finding him. He is not at Cheltenham now; he is at Bath; though Cheltenham is his general place of residence. Major Piper is a retired Indian officer, well known and respected."

And the account of the interview may possibly read less complicated if related as it took place, instead of as repeated by Mr. Meath.

He saw Major Piper at his lodgings at Bath: a little man, who had one of his gouty feet swathed in flannel. Mr. Meath disclosed his business, and put the malachite and gold sleeve-link into his hands. The Major recognised it at once, and smiled with pleasure.

"Ah," said he, "I don't forget this. It formed one out of a dozen, or so, small articles of value which disappeared from my dressing-case at Cheltenham under mysterious circumstances. It was about--yes--about four years ago. I had bought the jewellery in London, intending it as a present to my nephew on his twenty-first birthday. However, the very evening before it was to have been sent off, the things disappeared from my dressing-case."

"Had you any suspicions as to who could have taken them?" inquired Mr. Meath.

"No, I was utterly nonplussed: and am so still when I think of it," answered the Major. "I had some friends that night at my rooms, just enough to make up a couple of rubbers, all gentlemen of position who were more or less known to me. Early in the evening, when telling them what I had bought for my nephew, my man Tompkins brought in the dressing-case at my desire, and passed round the jewellery for the different guests to look at. After that, Tompkins took it away and put it back where he had found it--in one of the deep drawers in my dressing-table, but without locking it up; not, indeed, seeing any necessity for doing so. He----"

"I presume, sir, your man was trustworthy?" interrupted the listener.

"Perfectly so. Tompkins had been with me for years in India, and is with me still. The loss troubled him, I think, more than it troubled me. Not, of course, that I cared to lose the things!"

"Did any of the gentlemen enter your dressing-room during the evening?"

"Dear me, yes. It adjoined the sitting-room, and some of them were in and out. Candles were alight in it. Well, the next day, when the small case of jewellery came to be looked for, it was nowhere to be found; nor, so far as I am aware, has anything been heard of it from that day to this."

"Sir," said Mr. Meath, "was it possible that any person could have had access to your dressing-room in the course of the evening, while you and your visitors were busy at the card-table?"

"No, that could not be," answered Major Piper. "To get access to the dressing-room, they must have passed through the room where we sat, or else through a little anteroom on the other side of the dressing-room, and Tompkins sat in the ante-room the whole evening long."

"Did you put the matter into the hands of the police?" inquired Mr. Meath.

"I had it inquired into privately by the police," replied the Major, "but I would not allow it to be made public. On the one hand it was impossible for me to suspect my servant; while on the other I did not choose to have it thought that I suspected any of my guests. It was a most disagreeable affair, and worried me a good deal at the time. I was always hoping that something might turn up; but I suppose it has grown too late in the day to expect it now."

"I don't know that," said Mr. Meath. "This sleeve-link may prove the connecting link between your robbery and the still darker crime recently enacted at Heron Dyke: that is, it may lead to the discovery of both perpetrators, who may prove to have been one and the same man. Will you, sir, oblige me with the names of the gentlemen, so far as your memory serves, who made up your card-party on the night of the loss?"

"There can be no objection to my doing that," said the Major; "and I hope with all my heart it may prove of use to you. I can tell you every name, for the night and its doings lie with unfaded impression on my memory."

Mr. Meath took down the names from his dictation, as well as the date when the robbery occurred. They all appeared to be men of standing--most of them of undeniable connections.

"Two of them, Dr. Backhouse and my old comrade, Sir Marcus Gunn, are dead," remarked the Major. "Of the others, two are living in Cheltenham; one lives abroad, attaché to an embassy; and one or two have passed out of my knowledge. They may be living anywhere: the world is wide."

"Will you point out those one or two to me?" asked Mr. Meath--and Major Piper did so.

Such was the substance of the narrative Mr. Meath had now to relate at Heron Dyke.

"I have brought the list of names with me," he added to Mr. Conroy, when he finished. "Perhaps, sir, you and this lady will be good enough to look at it, and to tell me whether any one of the gentlemen is known in this neighbourhood."

Edward Conroy took the paper handed to him, and ran his eyes over the list, but without the least expectation of finding on it any name that he should recognise. Mr. Meath watched him with a kind of suppressed eagerness.

"'Admiral Tamberlin,'" read out Conroy, in a muttered tone, "'Doctor Backhouse, Sir Gunton Cleeve----'" and, before speaking the next name, he came to a dead standstill. Mr. Meath, the suppressed eagerness still in his eyes, smiled grimly to himself when he saw Conroy's start of surprise.

For a moment Conroy stared at the name, which he had not yet spoken, in speechless amazement. Then, recovering himself, he passed the paper to Miss Winter without a word, simply pointing with his forefinger to the name.

"Oh, impossible!" exclaimed Ella, her tone full of fright, her face turning white as death.

"Madam," interposed Mr. Meath, detecting her emotion, "it does not follow that because a gentleman may have been wearing these sleeve-links now, he was the one to steal them from Major Piper. The thief may have sold them, and he bought them legitimately."

"But see you not, sir," cried Ella, grasping the case mentally, "that if this gentleman made one of the Major's guests that evening, and it was he who lost the link in the struggle here with Hubert Stone----"

She paused, unable to continue. Mr. Meath slowly nodded his head.

"Yes, madam, I see the difficulties--if this gentleman is indeed known here----"

"Known here! why, he lives here," interrupted Ella. "Oh, Edward, it cannot, cannot be!"

"My dear, you go to Mrs. Toynbee," whispered her lover. "Say nothing to her. Leave me to deal with this."

"But, Edward--surely you will not accuse him!" she cried aloud.

"Of course I will not. It may be that this dreadful suspicion can be cleared away. Mr. Meath"--looking at that able man--"must make it his business to ascertain first of all, if he can, whether grounds for accusing him exist."

And, opening the door for her to pass out, Conroy resumed his seat at the table.

Again Mr. Meath left the Hall as quietly as he had entered it. Edward Conroy joined the ladies, and found that not a word had been spoken to Mrs. Toynbee. He stayed to dine with them.

The winter afternoon had deepened to a still, close evening, when Mr. Conroy once more took his way to the north wing--for his watchings there had not ceased--before quitting the Hall for the night. The incident of the afternoon had disturbed him greatly, while Miss Winter felt thoroughly upset. His thoughts were bent upon it as he passed silently through the passages: of Katherine Keen this night he never once thought. Perambulating the still and deserted corridors, his mind utterly preoccupied, he came last of all to the gallery. He knew every nook and corner of the wing by this time, and could find his way about it in the dark almost as readily as by daylight. In one corner of the gallery was an old oak chair, and on this he now sat down, almost without being aware of what he did. Meath's news was working in his brain, bringing him disquiet and perplexity.

He might have sat for five minutes or for twenty, he could not tell which afterwards, when the deathlike silence that brooded over the place was suddenly broken. All at once a low, sweet, wailing voice spoke through the darkness--a woman's voice, with tears in it: "Oh! why don't you come to me? How much longer must I wait?"

Only those few words, and then utter silence again. Conroy started to his feet with an exclamation of surprise. He had been so immersed in his sombre meditations, he was so utterly taken unawares, that he was altogether at a loss to know from which direction the voice had come, whether from the right hand or the left, whether from above or below. He stood without moving for what seemed to him a number of minutes, hoping to hear the voice again, or the sound of footsteps, or some other token of a living presence; but in vain he listened. He heard a far-away door clash faintly in another wing of the house, but nothing more. He was alone with the silence and the darkness.

By-and-by, when convinced that his remaining there longer would be useless, he went slowly down the dark, shallow stairs which led below. It would never do to tell Ella in what manner he had been disturbed. She had enough of other troubles to occupy her thoughts at present.

None the less was Edward Conroy determined to fathom the mystery of the north wing; if it were possible for man to do so.

CHAPTER VII.

A STRANGER AT THE ROSE AND CROWN

Mrs. Carlyon sat in the breakfast-room of her pleasant house at Bayswater, planning out in her own mind the route she should take on her journey to Hyères, for which place she intended to depart ere many days had elapsed, when the morning letters were brought in. One of them was from her niece, Ella Winter. Mrs. Carlyon opened it, and sat transfixed at the news it contained: nothing less than an avowal from that young lady that she was engaged to be married to Edward Conroy.

The shock and surprise sent Mrs. Carlyon into Norfolk. She gave orders to her maid, Higson, to prepare for their instant departure.

"And it is just as well that I should go on another score," she told herself, as she stepped into her carriage to be driven to the station: "to ascertain whether my niece has relinquished that most absurd idea of hers--that she is not her Uncle Gilbert's legal inheritor. What a ridiculous world we live in!"

So, at a late hour that same evening, Mrs. Carlyon, with her maid, arrived at Heron Dyke--without any notice.

"Your letter, Ella, took my breath away," she began, hardly allowing herself a moment for greetings. "Has this engagement which you tell me of really gone so far that it cannot be broken off?"

"But who wants it to be broken off, Aunt Gertrude?" returned Ella.

"What! Consider, my dear--a newspaper reporter, for Mr. Conroy is neither more nor less than that. A very nice gentlemanly young man, I admit, and one who has made himself a name in a certain way, but scarcely a match for the heiress of Heron Dyke."

"I am not going to marry for ambition, aunt, but for--for----"

"Love, I conclude you would say. Love may be all very well in its way, but why not have combined the two? Your husband ought to be at least your equal in position. With your fortune and good looks, you might have aspired to marry into the peerage; at the very least, you ought to have a husband with a seat in Parliament. I am very much disappointed," concluded Mrs. Carlyon, sitting down on the nearest chair.

"I am sorry for that, aunt; and so will Mr. Conroy be."

"My dear! Surely you will not be so foolish as to tell him," cried Mrs. Carlyon, hastily. "What I say to you is strictly between ourselves. I like Mr. Conroy very well--I like him so well that I should not care to hurt his feelings, although he has ambitiously cast his eyes on you."

"I am afraid, aunt, he could not help liking me. He said so."

"I dare say! Well, perhaps that may be true. If he were but well-connected-- or a landed proprietor, say--or even a rising man in the law courts--or, in short, almost anything but a newspaper reporter, there is no one I would sooner see you marry. But as he is----"

"I am quite satisfied with him as he is, Aunt Gertrude. And you must please remember," added Ella, with a quaint little smile, "that it was at your house I first met him. Don't you remember with what *empressement* you introduced him to me? He was quite the lion of the evening: you made him so: still, of course, as you say, he was only a newspaper reporter."

Mrs. Carlyon fidgeted in her chair.

"One may be gratified to receive a person as a visitor," she said, "but it does not follow that one cares to make him a member of one's family. As to that evening, I have hated to think of it ever since, for it was when my jewels were stolen, and now I shall hate it still more. But, to return to the point, you, the mistress of Heron Dyke----"

"Am I the true mistress of Heron Dyke?--or, rather, shall I continue to be?" interrupted Ella.

"I will not hear a word of that nonsense," flashed Mrs. Carlyon. "My dear, I speak of you as you are: and I say that it is positively not seemly for a young lady in your position to wed a poor newspaper reporter."

"Ella put her arms round her aunt's neck and kissed her."

"Worldly-wise maxims do not come with a good grace from your lips, Aunt Gertrude," she whispered. "I have heard you say many a time that your marriage was one of pure affection, but I have never heard you say that you regretted it. You must let me be happy in my own unambitious way."

Mrs. Carlyon sighed. How differently the young and the old look at things!- -and how impossible it is to reconcile the views. Not that she regretted her own choice: and she supposed she should have to put up with this one. Ella was her own mistress, under no control.

"Is it quite irrevocable, my love?"

"I think so, auntie dear. You can ask Mr. Conroy."

Irrevocable Mrs. Carlyon found it to be. After a short while given to private lamentation, she resolved to make the best of it; and she did so with a good grace. One very powerful advocate in her mind was Edward Conroy himself.

She could not help liking him, admiring him; she mentally acknowledged that were she a young woman with a virgin heart, it would have been lost to Conroy. After frankly telling him that she did not approve of the match on account of his want of position, but that she could not and should not take any steps to hinder it, she became pleasant with him as before. Conroy received the rebuke with becoming humility: but he did not offer to relinquish Miss Winter.

Now that she was at Heron Dyke, Mrs. Carlyon determined to remain. With Mr. Conroy at the Hall every day, she considered it her duty to be at hand to afford proper countenance and support to Ella. Mrs. Toynbee was all very well, but she was not a relative: and duty was duty with Mrs. Carlyon. Her cough must take its chance this winter. It was possible that the bracing air of the east coast might prove as beneficial to her in the long-run as the sun-warmed but relaxing breezes of Southern France. And so she settled down in the old house, to stay there as long as might be expedient.

When Mr. Charles Plackett was at Heron Dyke, he had promised to write to Miss Winter as soon as he had communicated with his client of Nunham Priors. Instead of Charles Plackett writing, Mr. Denison himself wrote, and the following is what he said:

"Nunham Priors.

"MY DEAR YOUNG KINSWOMAN,

"You have often been in my thoughts since I saw you in London, now some weeks ago, and I look forward with great pleasure to your promised visit to me at Nunham Priors next spring.

"When in town last week I saw my lawyer, Charles Plackett, who gave me a long account of his visit to you at Heron Dyke. That visit was undertaken by him solely on his own responsibility, and without first consulting me, as he ought to have done. I have the utmost confidence in Plackett's good sense and business qualifications, but whether I should have sanctioned his visiting you for such a purpose is a question I will not now enter upon. What has been done, cannot be undone; and all I can now do, my dear, is to thank you, and express to you the admiration I feel for the frank and candid spirit in which you met his inquiries. As I told Plackett, many people under such circumstances would have shown him the door: I myself should probably have done so.

"Were I in your place, my dear young lady, I should stir no further in the matter respecting which Plackett called upon you. You have done everything that honour demands, and more than could be expected of you under the circumstances. Moreover, it appears to me that--though I admit one cannot help entertaining doubts--any further investigation would probably bring forth no results whatever. Let the affair rest: that is my advice to you. I have no particular ambition to be the master of Heron Dyke, especially now that I have learnt to know and love--aye, love, my dear--her who is its mistress. I have fortune enough and to spare, both for myself and that scapegrace boy who will succeed me. Why crave for more? A very little while and I must leave it, however much or however little it may be.

"Don't forget that I shall expect you at Nunham Priors in spring; and so for the present no more.

"From your affectionate kinsman,

"Gilbert Denison."

"P.S.--I am expecting Frank home in a week or two. I shall try to chain him by the leg until you come. I am anxious that you and he should be well acquainted with one another."

"Oh, indeed!" exclaimed Conroy, as he read this letter with an amused smile, for Miss Winter handed it to him when he came to the Hall on the morning she received it.

"It is evident Mr. Denison has made up his mind that you should fall in love with this mythical son of his."

She nodded.

"After all, Ella, would not that seem to be a most sensible arrangement? It would unite the two branches of the family and concentrate the property of both. What a pity you have given away your heart to the wrong man!"

"I begin to think so too," gravely answered Ella. "It may not be too late to reclaim the poor thing and give it as you suggest."

"It is never well to be rash. Had you not better await the return of this wandering relative? Perhaps he might not value the offering?"

"But if he should value it?"

"He may not value it as--as its present possessor does."

"I dare say he would, sir."

"In that case, should you wish to reclaim it, you shall have it back."

Ella glanced up. "Do you mean what you say? Is it a bargain?"

"Undoubtedly." And, Mr. Conroy appeared to speak without reservation.

"Is he tiring of me?" thought Ella.

"Shall you take Mr. Denison's advice, and let the matter of the succession drop?" resumed Conroy, after a pause.

"Certainly not. You would not wish me to, would you?"

"No. I think if any fraud was enacted, it should be traced out and exposed. I have always said so. But, do you know *why* I have chiefly wished it?"

"Why have you?"

"For your own peace, dear. I see you will have none until the matter shall be set at rest."

"That is true; that is true," she impressively answered. "But, oh, Edward, what can we do? What can we do more than we have already done?"

"Nothing--that I see at present. It does not much matter, one way or the other."

"Do you mean that my title to the estate, or non-title, does not matter?"

"Not much, I say."

"I do not understand you this morning, Edward."

Conroy smiled. "You will understand me better sometime."

"That I am sure I never shall--if I am to marry that young Denison."

"Yes, you will, despite young Denison," returned Conroy, the same provoking smile still upon his lips.

It was known that Mrs. Ducie had been suffering from a severe cold. Suddenly, without bidding good-bye to anyone, she started for London: with the object, as was understood, of obtaining better medical advice. Nullington hoped she would obtain that, and be restored to health, for she was rather a favourite.

Mrs. Ducie did not return; and the next piece of news heard was that her well-known miniature phaeton, together with its pair of ponies, had been bought by Lord Camberley and presented to his aunt, the Hon. Mrs. Featherstone. From this, gossips argued, Mrs. Ducie's return to Nullington seemed a somewhat problematical event. Captain Lennox--who appeared to have taken up his abode in London, paying The Lilacs a flying visit now and then, in by the night-train and away again in the morning--was questioned upon the point. He said Mrs. Ducie continued very unwell indeed; he was not sure but she would have to go abroad; if so, he might perhaps accompany her.

It might have been from this item of problematical news that a report got about that the Captain was also about to leave Nullington. He himself neither denied it nor affirmed it: it would depend, he said, on his sister's health.

One evening, when the Captain had come down for a rather longer stay than usual now, he went into the billiard-room at the Rose and Crown. Lennox was a man who could not exist without society, or spend an evening at home with no company but his own.

After the Captain had played a few games with young Mr. Sandys, of Denne Park, and was about to quit the hotel, the landlord, Butterby, drew him aside.

"Can I speak with you a moment, sir?"

"Well?" cried the Captain, shortly.

"Pardon me, Captain, for asking; but would you mind telling me whether there's any truth in the report that you are about to leave The Lilacs?"

"What if there should be, eh?" asked the Captain, with a quick, suspicious glance at his questioner.

"Why simply this, sir," replied the landlord, "that I think I know of somebody who might perhaps take it off your hands, furniture and all."

"Oh, indeed! Who's that?" asked the Captain.

"A Mr. Norris, sir, who is stopping in the hotel. He says----"

"What's his business here?"

"Nothing in particular, sir: halted here quite promiscuous yesterday; been going about a bit to see places. He's not a gentleman by any means," added the landlord. "I hope I know a gentleman when I see one, Captain; but he seems to have plenty of money. Retired from business, I should put it. Says he should like to settle down in this part of the country, for it takes his fancy, and is on the look-out for what he calls a 'quiet little shanty' that would suit himself and his two grown up daughters. So I thought, Captain, that if----"

"I understand," interrupted Lennox in his quick way. He paused for a moment or two, biting his lip, his eyes bent on the ground.

"He looks awfully ill," was the landlord's unspoken thought, as he stood watching him. "But I suppose he goes the pace when he's in London. It's sure to tell on a man in the long-run."

"It might be worth my while to see this Mr. Norris in the morning," said Lennox, breaking out of his reverie. "To tell you the truth, Butterby, I *have* some notion of leaving Nullington."

"So we heard. But I'm sorry to hear you say so, sir."

"Nothing, however, is settled at present. You see my sister finds this part of the country a little too bleak for her, and I myself have been out of sorts for some time. We have some idea of travelling for a year or two. I shall see how she is when I next run up to town. We may perhaps come back here, after all."

"We shall miss you, sir, if you don't," spoke Butterby.

Captain Lennox looked undecided: as if he could not make up his mind. A minute or two passed before he spoke.

"You might take an opportunity, Butterby, of sounding this guest of yours as to what kind of place it is that he really wants. The Lilacs might be too small for him, or two expensive--it might not suit him in many ways. In that case my seeing him on the matter would be useless. I will look round in the morning about ten o'clock, and then you can tell me the result."

With that, Captain Lennox adjusted the camellia in his buttonhole, lighted a fresh cigar, linked his arm in the arm of young Sandys, and went his way.

Captain Lennox was punctual. The clock was striking ten the next morning as he walked into the bar of the Rose and Crown. The landlord met him with a smiling face.

"Mr. Norris would like to see you, sir," he began. "I had a little talk with him last night; and, from what I can make out, if you can come to terms yours will be just the place to suit him. He's a little bit odd in some of his ways, but a pleasant party enough when you come to converse with him."

"You can show me to his room."

Mr. Norris was a tall, ungainly, big-boned man, dressed somewhat after the fashion of a middle-aged country squire of sporting proclivities, with cutaway coat, gaiters, blue-and-white neck-tie and high collar. But his clothes sat awkwardly upon him, and he seemed ill at ease in them. He rose up from the breakfast-table as Lennox entered the room, and waved him to a chair.

"Proud to see you, sir," he said. "Shall be at your service in two minutes. Am late this morning."

"Don't hurry yourself," said Captain Lennox, politely. But Mr. Norris rang the bell and had the tray taken away. He then drew his chair a little nearer the fire, so that he might face his guest, and spread his big bony hands out to the cheerful blaze.

"I'm told, sir, that you have a little shanty you are about to vacate," he said, "and as I'm in want of something of the kind we may perhaps strike a bargain."

"Possibly so, Mr. Norris. But it might be waste of time to go into any details before you have seen the place. I may tell you that there are three years of the lease still to run, and that I should like the furniture to be taken at a valuation."

"All right, Captain. If the place suits me we shan't quarrel about terms, I dessay. When shall I pay you a visit?"

"The sooner the better. I am due in London to-morrow. How would two o'clock to-day suit you? You would then have time to look over the cottage before dusk, and you might favour me with your company at dinner afterwards, if not otherwise engaged. It may take some little time to talk over preliminaries."

"All right, Captain, I'm your man. At two sharp I'll be with you."

Mr. Norris was as good as his word. A fly deposited him at The Lilacs at the time appointed, where he found Captain Lennox waiting. The Captain went with him over the premises. Mr. Norris made a very minute inspection of the place, peering into every nook and corner, and examining every cupboard and pantry in the house. About the condition of the furniture he did not seem to trouble himself.

"It's good enough for me and my lasses," he said, with a wave of one of his large hands, when Lennox observed that he was afraid the drawing-room carpet was rather well worn.

Last of all, the garden and grounds were thoroughly perambulated.

"I like everything I've seen," said Mr. Norris, as they went back indoors, "but before giving a final answer, I must hear what my two lasses have to say. It's to be their home as well as mine, you know, Captain. Just now they are in the West of Ireland, but they'll be back in a week from to-day."

"In a week, eh?"

"Perhaps you don't care to wait so long as that for my answer?"

The Captain replied that a week more or a week less was a matter of very slight importance to him. So it was left at that.

When dinner was announced, Lennox sat down with his guest and was studiously polite, though he did not seem to be in much humour for talking.

Mr. Norris, however, so far as he was concerned, did not let the conversation flag, while doing ample justice to the good things before him. He allowed no hint to drop as to what his profession in life had been or was now; but from certain things he said Lennox came to the conclusion that he was a man who had seen a good deal of the world, and had been acquainted with several phases of life of a more or less curious kind. Dinner over, young Sandys and three or four other men dropped in; there was an adjournment to the smoking-room, and after a time some one suggested cards.

"Do you play, Mr. Norris?" asked Lennox, with an air of languid interest.

"When I was a lad at home we used to play loo and speculation for nuts at Christmas time, and since then I've sometimes played a rubber of whist, but nothing more," answered Mr. Norris, with his broad smile. "Still, I'm no spoil-sport, and if one of you will only give me a lesson or two I'll do my best."

Mr. Sandys kindly undertook the part of mentor, and found his pupil a most apt one. In about ten minutes he said rather drily, "And now, I think, Mr. Norris, you will be quite able to take care of yourself," at which Mr. Norris nodded his head.

During the early part of the evening the luck seemed decidedly against Mr. Norris. But by-and-by there came a change, and his lost sovereigns began to find their way back to his pocket. It appeared to be a peculiarity of this Mr. Norris, that whenever he sustained a more severe loss than ordinary he leant back in his chair and gave vent to a hearty guffaw; whereas, when the cards happened to be in his favour and the pool fell to him, he looked as glum as a judge. Young Sandys stared at him through his eye-glass as though he were some strange animal who had found his way there by mistake, while Captain Lennox's cold, keen glances began to be directed more and more frequently towards his guest. It was dawning on the Captain's mind that Mr. Norris was, perhaps, not so much of a novice as he had tried to make himself out to be. At the close of the evening he rose from the table a winner to a small amount.

Norris was the first to leave. He bowed his awkward bow to the company generally, and shook hands with the Captain.

"Everything shall be settled in a week from now," he whispered with a meaning look. "Rely upon that. Good-night."

"Queer fish that," said young Sandys, as the door closed on Mr. Norris's lanky figure.

"Not quite the greenhorn he would have had us believe," remarked Gray, another of the guests. "Where the deuce did you pick him up, Lennox?"

"I'm glad he's gone," said Lennox, with an air of weariness, as he dropped into a chair "The fellow is after this place--if I should make up my mind to leave it."

"I say, old fellow, how jolly bad you look to-night!" said Downes Dyson as he proceeded to shuffle the cards.

"Yes, I'm altogether out of sorts. These horrible English winters are enough to kill anyone."

Captain Lennox was indeed glad that Mr. Norris had gone, and he would have been well pleased were he never going to see him again. He had contracted a great dislike for him, for which he could give no reasonable account to himself; a sort of dread which had grown deeper and deeper as the evening had advanced.

And he could not shake it off. His dreams that night were troubled ones: through the whole of them the tall, gaunt figure of Mr. Norris loomed ominously. Even in his sleep he felt that he hated him.

Next morning the Captain rose unrefreshed, and started by an early train for London. He was thinking that he needed a different air from the English air just as greatly as his sister did.

It was at the Rose and Crown that Mr. Conroy stayed when at Nullington. He and Norris had once or twice met on the stairs, and passed each other as strangers. On the evening above-mentioned, however, when Mr. Conroy was just about to go to rest, a tap came to the door of his sitting-room, and Norris appeared at it.

"I thought I'd just see whether you had retired yet, sir, having a word to say to you."

"Ah, is it you, Mr. Meath?" said Conroy. "Come in. You have some news for me, I presume. Sit down. What is it?"

"The news I have at present, sir, is this: that I have made some very curious discoveries indeed respecting the antecedents of the gentleman who goes by the name of Captain Lennox."

"*Goes* by the name! Is it not his real name?"

"Well, sir, he has gone by a lot of names in his time, but which of them's his real one is best known to himself."

From the breast-pocket of his coat, Mr. Meath drew a small memorandum-book, and opened it.

"Ten years ago," he began, "Lennox was passing under the name of Blaydon. At that time he was tuner to a large pianoforte firm in London. This situation he lost because a number of valuable articles were missed from different houses to which he was sent. We next hear of him under the name of Perke, as book-keeper at a fashionable hotel in Mayfair. Here also some robberies were perpetrated, but whether by him or not I am not in a position to assert. In any case, he lost his situation before long. After this he appears to have gone abroad for two or three years, and was seen in Paris, Brussels, Homburg, and other places. In some way or other, probably by successful gambling, he seems to have feathered his nest pretty considerably. We next find him at Cheltenham."

"At Cheltenham!" involuntarily exclaimed Conroy.

"At Cheltenham, sir. He had become Captain Lennox then, and was a very big card. Being Captain Lennox and a great swell, he is of course above peculations, unless some very tempting chance offers itself, as in the case of Major Piper's jewel-case. By his skill at cards and billiards he contrives to make a very comfortable income. He entices young men of fortune to his rooms, and there fleeces them. Do you follow me, sir?"

"Quite so."

"It would appear that he at length becomes fearful that Cheltenham is growing too warm for him; and he wisely beats a retreat from it before any suspicion touches him. Accompanied by his sister, Mrs. Ducie, he comes to Norfolk, and takes The Lilacs on a five or six years' lease. It would seem a curious, out-of-the-way place to come to," remarked Mr. Meath, looking off his note-book for a moment; "but no doubt Lennox knew what he was about, and I have very little doubt that the scheme has paid him handsomely. He must have known that there were many young men of family in this part of the country, some of them with more money than brains, and Captain Lennox having more brains than money was exactly the man to adjust the difference. It is a pity, sir, a great pity," added Mr. Meath, with a solemn shake of the head, "that so clever a rascal did not stop short at plucking pigeons, and leave the darker paths of villany untrodden. He might have gone on living as a gentleman and among gentlemen for years to come."

Edward Conroy had been thinking. There were some discrepancies in this history. "You speak of Lennox as a tuner of pianos and an hotel clerk, Mr. Meath; but he is undoubtedly a gentleman, both as regards education and manners. I think he must have been born one."

"Little doubt of that, sir. 'Tis but another edition of the old story, I take it. Well-connected parents, expensive bringing-up, perhaps good launch in life--perhaps not good through lack of funds: then temptation, weakness, ruin. Repudiated by friends, or perhaps friends dead. Then another start under a fresh name and from a lower rung of the ladder. Ah, my dear sir, such cases are unfortunately but too common. This is a queer world, yet men must live in it."

Conroy silently assented.

"How far do you suppose Mrs. Ducie has been implicated in these unpleasant matters?"

The private detective shook his head.

"Sir, I can't answer that. We have made no discovery against her as yet; neither do we care to push any. She is much attached to her brother, and she has clung to him in her sisterly affection. It can hardly be that she has lived without suspicion; any way, as to his making money by fleecing the world at cards. Whether she has known of worse things, I can't say. If so, one could not expect her to denounce him; but she must have walked upon thorns."

"I suppose she is really a widow?--and her name Ducie?

"Yes, sir, that's all straightforward enough. Her husband was an officer in the army; he died young, and left her with a fair income--which is hers still. People like her, and she has some good acquaintances. So has the Captain, for that matter."

"What do you purpose doing next?" asked Conroy.

"Well, sir, my next move--though I don't say when it will take place, either this day or that day--will be to apply for a search-warrant, and go quietly over The Lilacs--into every nook and corner of it."

"With any particular object in view?"

"Yes, sir, a very particular one. I hope to find there a malachite and gold sleeve-link, to match the one that was found upon the gravel at Heron Dyke."

Conroy almost smiled: this appeared to him to be so improbable a hope.

"You cannot expect to find it. Knowing, as he must have known, that he had lost the one sleeve-link in the struggle with Hubert Stone, Lennox's first care would be to effectually hide its fellow."

"Let me tell you, Mr. Conroy, that the chances are he *didn't*. These criminals are always making some fatal mistake; and that's a very common one--the not doing away effectually, as you are pleased to term it, sir, and it's an apt word, with the proofs that might destroy them."

CHAPTER VIII.

TOGETHER AT LAST

Sundry matters had been taking place concerning Philip Cleeve which might well have been told previously.

It was on a Wednesday morning, as may be remembered, that Philip started for London, on business, as Lady Cleeve was led to suppose, connected with Mr. Tiplady's office. On Thursday evening Lady Cleeve waited up to welcome her son's return. But Philip did not come.

"He must be staying in town to spend the evening with Mr. Bootle," she said to herself. "I shall have a letter in the morning."

The morning brought neither letter nor messages from the truant, and Lady Cleeve sent her breakfast away nearly untasted. "After all," she thought, "seeing that he will return to-day, he probably hardly thought it worth while to write."

But when Friday evening passed away and still Philip came not, and when Saturday morning's post brought her no letter, then Lady Cleeve became seriously alarmed. Business might, of course, be detaining him, she knew that; but why did he not write? And Philip, as she believed, was so ultra-dutiful.

"I will send to Mr. Tiplady, and risk it, she thought. She would have sent to inquire before, only Philip had so intense a dislike to being, what he called, looked after. Once, when he had stayed away at Norwich a day or two beyond the time of coming home, she had gone herself to the office to ask about him, and Philip was annoyed about it.

"Bridget," she said, calling to the maid who had waited upon her for many years, and who was as well known in Nullington as Lady Cleeve herself, "you had better go and inquire at the office when they expect Mr. Philip home. You can say, if you like, that I am a little uneasy at not hearing from him."

Away went Bridget, in her warm Scotch plaid shawl and black coal-scuttle bonnet. Mr. Tiplady was standing at the office-door, looking up and down the street. Bridget delivered to him her lady's message.

"Lady Cleeve sent you to me to inquire about the movements of Mr. Philip," cried the architect, after listening. "I was just going to send to ask Lady Cleeve the same question."

This famous architect, renowned in more counties than one, was a kindly, unpretending man, small and slight, and chary of speech in general. He took off his hat to push back the few scanty grey hairs left on his head, as he looked at the servant.

"My lady thought, sir, that you must know what was keeping Mr. Philip so long in London."

"I know nothing about it, Bridget. I don't know why he went. His absence is causing us some inconvenience."

Bridget, who was much in her mistress's confidence, could not make this out.

"He went upon business for you, sir, did he not?"

"Not at all. Mr. Best here got a note from him on Wednesday morning, saying he had to run up to town on a little business, but should be back the following day. We have heard nothing of him since. Make my compliments to your lady, and tell her this."

Lady Cleeve became actively alarmed now. All sorts of dire forebodings filled the mother's heart. London was a place beset with dangers in many ways: she had heard, and fully believed, that hardly a day passed but somebody or other was lost in it, and that they were never heard of again.

Sending out to order a fly, she was set down at the office. Mr. Tiplady was in his private room then, and handed her to a seat.

"I would be only too glad to tell you what is detaining him, if I knew," said the little man kindly, in answer to her somewhat impassioned appeal. "We supposed he had gone up upon some matter for yourself. Lost?--lost? no, no, dear Lady Cleeve; don't imagine anything so improbable as that. Philip is quite old enough to take care of himself."

"But what can he have gone to London for? And why should he have made a mystery of it?"

"Well, to say the truth, that's what I cannot quite understand. Best said a word to me this morning--he got it from young Plympton, I fancy--that Philip had been embarking money in some speculation, and---- Do you know anything about it?"

"Nothing," said Lady Cleeve, whose face was growing more anxious with every moment.

"I'll call Best in," said the architect.

But upon going into an adjoining room he found that Mr. Best had stepped out. So he brought in Richard Plympton. This young man, who had been placed in the architect's office as an "improver," was brother to Mr. Kettle's curate, and was a great friend of Philip.

Young Plympton, after shaking hands with Lady Cleeve, told what he knew, thinking it right under present circumstances to do so: that Philip had bought some shares in a rich silver-mining company, the Hermandad, and that he had gone up to town to see if he could not sell out again.

"Oh," said Mr. Tiplady, "embarked money in that, has he? I heard that same mine spoken of yesterday--quite incidentally."

"It is a very rich mine, is it not, sir?" cried young Plympton with enthusiasm.

"Very," drily responded the architect.

"Captain Lennox got him the shares, sir. He is one of the directors, and has gone in for it himself largely."

"Sorry for him," cried Mr. Tiplady. "The mine has come to grief."

"No!" exclaimed the young man, opening his eyes widely. "You don't mean that, sir! Then"--a thought striking him--"it must be that which has been keeping Lennox so much in town lately."

"Ay, no doubt. That will do, Mr. Plympton. I wonder whether Philip has risked much upon this worthless thing?" added the architect to Lady Cleeve, as his clerk withdrew.

"It is sad news for me," she sighed, wiping her pale face. "We can soon ascertain, by inquiring at the bank how much money he has drawn out. Of course, anything is better than that he should be lost."

"Of course," smiled Mr. Tiplady. "Still I don't myself see why this matter should be keeping Philip in London. It has been known to the public some days now. Shall I make the inquiry at the bank for you, Lady Cleeve?"

"If you will take the trouble. I shall be very much obliged to you."

"I may want your authority before they'll answer me. I'm not quite sure, though; they know me for Philip's good friend."

It was arranged that he should get into the fly now with Lady Cleeve. The driver was directed to stop at the bank. Mr. Tiplady went in, and came out with a serious face.

"Will they not answer you?" cried Lady Cleeve.

"Oh yes; they made no difficulty about that."

"Well! How much has he drawn out?"

"Nearly every pound he had there."

So poor Lady Cleeve had to go home with her anxiety augmented, instead of lessened. Suppose Philip, in his dismay at the loss of all his money, should--should have done something rash!

Saturday wore itself away. The look on the mother's face was pitiful to see. She sat at the window which faced the entrance-gate, looking for one that did not appear. And when dusk had closed in she still sat on in the same spot, listening in the dark with straining eyes for the well-known footfall that was so long in coming.

Sunday morning came and with it the postman, for there was an early postal delivery on that day at Nullington. But there was no letter from Philip. Dr. Spreckley was in the act of brushing his hat preparatory to setting out for church, when in rushed Bridget. Her lady had suddenly been taken with one of her old attacks, and the Doctor must hasten to her.

Dr. Spreckley had another patient on his hands at that time--the Reverend Francis Kettle; he was laid up with gout. When Dr. Spreckley called there after church, he mentioned Lady Cleeve's illness to Maria.

"She had been getting on so well lately," he lamented. "Anxiety of mind has brought on this attack; nothing else."

"Anxiety of mind?" repeated Maria.

"Yes; all about that harum-scarum son of hers. He went to London on Wednesday last, and has never been heard of since. She is in a fine quandary, I can tell you, fancying some dreadful harm has come to him."

"But why should harm come to him?" asked Maria, her heart beating wildly.

"Why, indeed! He does harm enough to himself without its coming to him gratuitously. Been and spent all his money; made ducks and drakes of it."

"Oh!" gasped Maria. "*How?*"

"How!" returned the Doctor. "Well"--looking at Maria's tale-telling countenance--"been embarking a lot of it in some precious mining scheme, and the mine has burst up."

Maria went to Lady Cleeve's that afternoon. She found her very ill. Maria hid her own fears and forebodings, and spoke cheerfully and hopefully; although every now and then a blinding rush of tears would come into her eyes when she thought that perhaps in very truth she should never see Philip more on this side the grave. More than ever before, she seemed to realise how dear he was to her heart.

How many days of this terrible anxiety went on, neither of them cared to number. The vicar was getting better now, though still confined to a sofa in his room, and Maria spent much of her time at Homedale. One morning there arrived a telegram addressed to Lady Cleeve. The poor mother's face turned paler still, and her hands trembled so much that she could not open it. She signed to Maria to take the paper.

"No. 6, Maxwell Terrace, Wandsworth, London.

"*From* PHILLIP CLEEVE,

"I have met with a slight accident, which will detain me in London for a few days yet. It is nothing serious, so do not be alarmed. Another message to-morrow."

"Thank heaven! my boy still lives," said Lady Cleeve. Tears of thankfulness stood in Maria's eyes: for she also had been fearing the worst. "And yet it is strange why he has not written," mused Lady Cleeve, stretching out her hand for the paper. "He says, 'Another message to-morrow!' Why send a telegram when, if he were to post a letter this evening, it would reach me in the morning? He must be worse than he wishes me to know of; he must be so ill that he cannot write. He may be dying. And I cannot go to him!"

"I will go to him, dear Lady Cleeve!" said Maria, with a lovely flush on her cheeks.

"You, my dear!"

"Yes, I. I can go: papa is almost well now."

"But, my dear child, will it do for *you* to go? You----"

"I am his promised wife, and who has more right to be by his side, at such a time as this, than I have?" She flung herself into Lady Cleeve's arms, and the two wept together.

Maria lost no time. Before the astonished vicar could say yes or no, before he quite understood what the matter was, she was on her way to the railway-station.

A cab stopped that same evening at the door of No. 6, Maxwell Terrace. Miss Kettle alighted, knocked, and inquired for Mr. Cleeve.

Before the servant had time to reply, a white-haired, ruddy-faced gentleman came out of a side-room. "Come inside, come inside," he said, as he peered at Maria through his spectacles. "Yes, Mr. Cleeve is under this roof. He is my guest, you know; and you, I presume, are some relation of his?" he added, as he led the way into the parlour. "Perhaps his sister?"

"No, not his sister," faltered Maria, the difficulties of her position suddenly presenting themselves to her. "I am not related to him."

"Not related to him!" repeated the old gentleman, gazing at her. But, there was something so benevolent in the ruddy face, so kindly in the honest eyes, that Maria took heart and courage.

"I am his promised wife, sir," she said simply. "There was nobody but me to come."

"His promised wife, now! Bless my heart, but that's very nice, do you know! I never had a promised wife; I often wish that I had. My name's Marjoram, my dear--Josiah Marjoram, late of Bucklersbury, City; now retired, with nothing to do--nothing to do. It's hard work, though, sometimes."

"But about Philip--about Mr. Cleeve, sir?" said Maria, earnestly. "Is he very ill? I was to send a telegram to his mother if I got here in time. How was he hurt?"

"Sit down, my dear, and I will tell you all about it. It was as gallant a thing as ever I saw. I was standing at my drawing-room window one afternoon, whistling to myself, and thinking about nothing in particular, when all at once a hansom cab came dashing round the corner at a most furious rate. A little child was running across the road: it stumbled and fell: upon which a young man, who happened to be passing, and whom I had not noticed before, dashed into the road and seized the child in his arms. But he was too late; the cab was over him. The child escaped with a few bruises, but the young man was--well, let us put it, rather badly hurt. 'Take him to the hospital,' called out the people, running up. 'The only hospital he shall go to is my house,' I said to them: and into it he was carried. We found a name on some cards in his pocket-book, 'Mr. Cleeve,' but no address, so that I was unable to communicate with his friends."

"And he was too much injured to give you the address!" exclaimed Maria.

"Just so; he was not sufficiently sensible. But he is getting better now; oh, very much better," added the old gentleman, briskly. "As a proof of it, it was he who dictated the telegram to Lady Cleeve this morning. My doctor and the one from London both say that with care we shall soon have him on his legs again now."

"I should like to see him, sir, if you please," said Maria, faintly.

"So you shall, my dear: so you shall, when I have spoken to the nurse. Meanwhile, my housekeeper, Mrs. Wale, a good, motherly old soul, shall show you to your room, to take your bonnet off. We prepared it for his mother, thinking she might come."

The old housekeeper came in curtseying. She supposed Maria to be Lady Cleeve's daughter. Maria took off her travelling things, and was then ready to see Philip. Mr. Marjoram opened the chamber-door for her. She caught sight of a white face on the pillow, and two preternaturally large eyes, that stared at her as if she were a visitor from the dead. She bent her face to his.

"Oh, my dear one!" she murmured. "Thank Heaven, I have found you at last!" And Maria made up her mind that she would not leave him again. The doctors said that very much would depend on good nursing. Maria felt that no one could nurse him as she could; at least, she would help to do it. The old gentleman approved of this so much that he clapped his hands in applause; he told Maria he wished she could be converted by some good fairy into his real daughter, and never go away from his house.

On the morning after Philip's first wretched night in London, when he was somewhat restored to common sense, he resolved to return to Nullington and confess all his weakness and folly to his mother and to Mr. Tiplady. There was no help for it. But the thought struck him that he ought once more to go to the Hermandad office in the City, and to ascertain, if possible, whether the silver-mining prospect was absolutely hopeless.

The place was still shut up, and Philip could hear nothing. In coming away he met a gentleman whom he had seen at The Lilacs, an acquaintance of Captain Lennox and Mrs. Ducie. This gentleman had also put some money into the mine, and had come down to the City on the same errand as Philip.

"Lennox? No, I can't tell you where he is; I've not seen him here lately," he said, in answer to Philip's question. "Lennox is as hard hit as we are, I expect; worse, in fact. He may be staying with those friends he has at Wandsworth; he is there sometimes."

"Can you give me their address?

"Why, yes, I can. I spent an evening or two there with Lennox in the summer."

Philip took the address, and went to Wandsworth. He found the people, but could not hear anything of Captain Lennox; they supposed him to be at Nullington. It was after leaving their house that Philip met with the accident. It is probable that his previous night's vigil, and the troubled state his mind was in, rendered him less quick and agile than he might otherwise have been.

When Philip had gained sufficient strength, he poured into Maria Kettle's ear all the story of his folly and ruin, the latter culminating with these dreadful mines. He was yet so weak and ill that when he had done he cried like a child. Maria pressed his hand to her soft, warm cheek, and soothed and comforted him.

"I think sometimes, Maria, that if you had not cast me off as you did all this would not have happened," he continued; "and yet how weak and foolish I have been all through, no one knows better than myself."

"I will never leave you again," she murmured, with scarlet cheeks: and they sealed the promise with a kiss.

"I shall always say, Maria, your father was harder to me than he need have been."

"Yes. But the truth is, Philip, he has had more on his mind than he would speak of," she returned. "It was about----"

"About, what?" queried Philip, as she stopped.

"I am almost ashamed to mention it."

"I shall never rest now, till you have told me."

"Papa took up a notion that you were somehow concerned in those robberies which took place: his own purse, you know--and the Doctor's snuff-box--and the jewels."

Philip's large eyes grew larger as he stared at Maria.

"Not that I stole them? You can't mean that!"

"I fear that he was afraid you did. Dr. Downes was also."

Philip lay without speaking, lost in astonishment. Presently he burst into the strongest laugh his feeble state allowed.

"What a joke, Maria! They could not believe such a thing of me. I am Philip Cleeve."

The words imparted their own assurance. Though Maria had never needed to be assured.

"Did *you* think this?"

"Oh, Philip! Don't you know me better than that?"

"My dear, yes. Forgive the question. You say you will never leave me again, Maria: I bless you for that. If we could but be married here, and now, so that no adverse fate might ever more part us! Here and now!"

Maria's vivid blush was the only answer.

"But how could we live now that our future is marred?" continued Philip. "As Tiplady's partner, I could have ensured you a good home; but the money which was to have secured that position, the twelve hundred pounds, is gone for ever."

"I have two thousand pounds that I think you have not heard of, Philip," she said in a low tone, as she hid her face. "Mrs. Page left it to me. We will pay over some of it to Mr. Tiplady, in place of that which is lost."

"Maria!"

"Yes," she answered. "I have been intending it ever since I knew you were getting better. Do not fret after the money, Philip. Captain Lennox is worse off----"

"Hang Captain Lennox!" interjected Philip. "But for him I should never have got into trouble of any kind."

"He had embarked, it is said, a great deal in this mine," added Maria. "People fancy that it is his loss in it which makes him think of giving up The Lilacs."

Romantic though old Mr. Marjoram showed himself to be, it yet may have surprised him to be told that the two young people enjoying his hospitality had determined to get married as soon as possible, while Philip still lay ill and helpless--if he, the kind old gentleman, would only help them to accomplish it.

"Oh ho!" said he. "Love's young dream, and all that, eh? Your parents have destined you for one another from childhood, you tell me."

"That's quite true," said Philip, from his pillow.

"Philip will need careful tending for some time to come, as you know, sir," spoke Maria, with soft red cheeks and downcast eyes; "and no one can tend him as a wife can. If you, sir, would be at the trouble of procuring a special license for us, and--and Philip and I thought if you would not mind our being married here quietly some morning----"

Tears twinkled on the old gentleman's eyelashes. He drew Maria to him and pressed her to his heart, and she cried a little on his shoulder as she might have done on that of her father. Mr. Marjoram wished that Heaven had given him such a child.

Thus it fell out that a few days later a quiet wedding took place in the drawing-room of No. 6, Maxwell Terrace. Philip was lifted out of bed that day for the first time since his accident, and lay on a couch while the ceremony was performed. He looked desperately white and ill, poor fellow! but the light of perfect content shone in his eyes, and the old sweet smile that used to mark the Philip Cleeve of old days came and went continually on his lips. Mr. Marjoram gave away the bride, and his sister, a charming maiden lady of fifty, came all the way from Hertford to countenance the ceremony. And the old state of things then went on again. Poor helpless Philip lay in bed, and Maria waited on him.

But he seemed to get rapidly better now. And when sufficiently well to leave the good old man's hospitable roof, he and Maria went to a quiet seaside place lying on their way to Norfolk, that Philip might inhale the refreshing sea-breezes for a few days before returning home. At present he and his wife would stay with Lady Cleeve.

She, Lady Cleeve, was thankful in her heart for all that had happened, now that it had led to all this happiness. The Vicar, making up his mind at first to be very stern and high and mighty, broke down at the first interview. For one thing, his mind was at rest as to Philip's fancied participation in the robberies. Too much proof had been found at The Lilacs by Mr. Detective Meath, to admit of suspicion against anyone but Captain Lennox.

Dr. Downes's snuff-box had turned up first. It was supposed the Captain had been afraid to get rid of it for a time. Most of the jewels lost at Heron Dyke had been found there; and--the fellow sleeve-link of malachite and gold.

"That we must have a snake-in-the-grass amongst us here, I knew," cried Dr. Downes; "but I never suspected Lennox. I was more inclined to suspect *you*, Master Philip," with a nod at Philip, who was lying on a sofa, "although you are your father's son and your good mother's. You are laughing, are you? Well, you can afford to laugh, things having turned out so: you'd have found it no laughing matter had you been the black sheep."

"I dare say not, Doctor," answered Philip.

"But it is an awful thought that he, Lennox, whose hand has been meeting ours in friendship, should have been the murderer of Hubert Stone."

CHAPTER IX.

IN THE DUSK OF EVENING

Never had the good people of Nullington had more food for gossip, wonder, and surmise--never had they been so startled out of the ordinary quietude of their lives, as during the Christmastide to which events have now brought us. The marriage, under somewhat romantic circumstances, of Philip Cleeve, and the coming home of himself and his bride, would, in ordinary times, have served as the chief topic of conversation for a month to come. But this comparatively tame episode was completely overshadowed by the startling revelations in connection with Captain Lennox.

Both Captain Lennox and his sister had vanished as completely as if the earth had swallowed them up. They had been traced to London, but there the trail was lost, and it had not hitherto been found again. Lennox had never come back to complete the arrangements respecting the letting of the cottage to Mr. Norris. Something must have aroused his suspicions, and some one, probably one of his own servants, must have sent him timely information respecting the execution of the search-warrant. In any case, he was nowhere to be found after that day. Mr. Meath was at fault; the general police were at fault; and meanwhile the cottage remained in charge of the police local constabulary.

Christmas at Heron Dyke could not well have been spent more quietly. Conroy was away for a few days about this time. Mrs. Carlyon and Ella went into the town occasionally to see Maria and Philip, and that was about their only dissipation.

"It must have been Captain Lennox who took the jewel-case out of my dressing-room that night at Bayswater," remarked Mrs. Carlyon one day. "And to think I could not get rid of an uneasy suspicion that it might have been poor Philip Cleeve who had taken it!"

Ella looked up in surprise.

"Philip Cleeve!" she exclaimed.

"Well, yes; I am ashamed to say so, Ella."

"But what could possibly have led you to such a suspicion as that, Aunt Gertrude?"

"Captain Lennox led me. Otherwise I should no more have thought of Philip in the matter than I should have thought of you."

Ella felt bewildered.

"Surely Captain Lennox did not dare to accuse Philip!"

"Oh dear, no. One day, a few weeks after the loss, when Captain Lennox was in town and calling upon me, he inquired whether the jewels had been found. In talking of the affair, he dropped a word--it was little more than one--which somehow turned my thoughts to Philip. The Captain caught it up again--as if he had let it drop inadvertently, and I did not pursue it. Since then, when I have heard at times how fast Philip was supposed to be spending money at cards, billiards, and such like, that inadvertent word has returned to my mind doubtfully and most disagreeably."

"Do you suppose Captain Lennox wished you to think he accused Philip?"

"No," replied Mrs. Carlyon. "I think he wanted to instil a slight doubt of his possible guilt into my mind, so as to more completely throw any possible suspicion off himself. That is how I fancy it must have been."

"Aunt Gertrude," said Ella, musingly, "I wonder whether it was Captain Lennox who stole Freddy Bootle's watch and chain that same night--and then made out that his own purse was likewise stolen?"

"Little need to wonder! nothing was ever much more sure than that," said Mrs. Carlyon. "The man must have lived by these peculations. And to think what a gentleman he was through it all!"

Conroy came back. And whatever minor elements of disquietude might make themselves felt now and again, there was a certain sweet fulness of content about Ella's life just now, that nothing could seriously affect. She had won the sweetest guerdon a woman can win, and all things else, whether pleasing or displeasing, seemed dwarfed in comparison with that one supreme fact. The more she saw of Conroy, the more she seemed to find in him to love and appreciate. Day by day the choice she had made approved itself more fully to her heart. Even Mrs. Carlyon, now that she was domesticated daily with Conroy, no longer wondered at what she called Ella's infatuation.

It had been arranged that the marriage should take place early in spring. Ella wished to delay the event until the doubt as to the date of her uncle's death, and her own rightful inheritance of the property, should be cleared up; but Mr. Conroy urged that that was no good cause for delay.

"Suppose," she said to him one day, "that after we are married it should be discovered that I am not the true heiress, and Heron Dyke goes from me?"

"What then?" he answered. "We should still have enough for comfort. You possess some income that is indisputably your own; and I dare say I could match it, in one way or another."

"By your newspaper work?"

"By that or other things. I have given up the newspapers for the present: am not sure that I shall take to them again. Be at rest, my dear, and trust to me. We shall be able to keep up a modest home, and a cow, and a pony-carriage. What more can we want?"

"You are laughing at me, Edward."

"No, indeed. I only wish you not to be troubled about this property. It may be yours, or it may not be."

"I fancy you think it is not mine?"

"I fancy that if everybody possessed their legal rights, it would turn out to be at this moment Mr. Denison's. But we have yet no proof of that, and it may be that I am mistaken."

"The shortest way would be to give it up to him at once."

"My dear, Mr. Denison would not take it; he is one of the last men in the world to do so."

"Do you know Mr. Denison?"

"I have seen him. I know that he is a straightforward, honourable man."

Ella sighed.. She wished the doubt could be solved.

Mr. Conroy wished the same, though perhaps in a less ardent way. It did not *trouble* him as it did her; he was more patient, more reconciled to let time work out its own ends. He held a secret conviction that Aaron was at the bottom of the plot, if there had been a plot; but Conroy kept that impression to himself.

Harsh, crabbed and unsympathetic as was Aaron Stone, both by nature and training, the shock of his grandson's sudden death, following so soon after that of the Squire, had not failed to leave its traces behind. In a few short months Aaron seemed to have grown a dozen years older. His hair was thinner and whiter, he had become more feeble in his gait, and he claimed the assistance of a stick in walking more frequently than before. He maundered in an undertone to himself as he walked about the Hall with his keys--his chief duty now was to shut up the old house at night and to open it in the morning; he did little else; and he would often speak out aloud as in answer to some question when nobody had asked him one. He would have liked to follow his mistress about much as a faithful old mastiff might have done, gazing from the doors when she was in the grounds, moving restlessly about her chair at dinner. To Conroy he had taken umbrage, and would mutter to himself that a strange man had no business at Heron Dyke; the best of 'em were but spies.

"What do he do up in that north wing so much?" soliloquised the old man in the homely speech he was pleased to indulge in when off duty. "I see him, evening after evening, a-creeping softly up and a-creeping down again. What do he do it for? What's he looking after? Do the young mistress know of it, I wonder? Who can answer for't that he warn't in that theft o' the jewels? Yah! Spies!"

Of all the inmates of the Hall, the one least tolerant of his crotchets and his failings was Mrs. Carlyon. On occasion she spoke of them to Ella.

"It is partly your fault, child; you give in to him so."

"I don't think I do, aunt. In what way do I?"

"In many ways. Look at that senseless fancy he has taken up of having no men-servants in the house but himself! And you fall in with it."

"We have enough maids for the work, Aunt Gertrude."

"I am aware of that--I suppose we have not much less than half-a-score here, including your maid and mine. That is not the question. In your position, mistress of this grand old place, it behoves you to keep men-servants as other people do. But because Aaron sets his face against it, you----"

"It is not that, aunt," interrupted Ella. "What I thought right to do I should do, in spite of Aaron; believe that. It is the uncertainty in which things are, that causes me to live quietly. Once I hear--if I ever do--that I am the rightful owner of Heron Dyke, you will find me make all changes that are suitable."

Mrs. Carlyon said no more then. She heartily wished her sojourn at Heron Dyke was at an end, that she might return to her own more comfortable home. For, in her opinion, the atmosphere of the Hall was not comfortable. Of that dark north wing she had a wholesome dread, as well as of the lost girl's spirit which was supposed to haunt it. To her niece she did not speak of this: but she and Mrs. Toynbee --who was very poorly at this time and kept much to her own chamber--talked confidentially together, and agreed that matters altogether were more doubtful than they ought to be.

"This is a queer thing, Miss Ella, that folks down at Nullington are whispering to one another," exclaimed Aaron, overtaking his mistress one afternoon in the new conservatory.

"What is it that they are whispering?" she turned to ask.

"About that Captain Lennox. If 'twas him that robbed the Hall, then he must have been the villain who destroyed my poor boy. Ah, ma'am, but it's a terrible world!"

"I fear some of us find it so, Aaron."

"To think of it! Captain Lennox! But I never liked him, ma'am. I never liked that sharp, foxy face of his."

Ella mentally wondered whom the old man had liked.

"I mistrusted him, Miss Ella, from the first time I saw him. When a man talks to you so soft and silky-like, as the Captain did, and at the same time fixes you with such a pair of cruel, hungry-looking eyes, it is best to have nothing to do with him. I set such a man down as dangerous."

Miss Winter had herself always felt a secret distrust of Lennox, without knowing the reason why. Perhaps, as Aaron had said, it was the contrast between his smooth, dulcet tones, and the expression in his cold, hard-set glances: any way, she had never taken cordially to Captain Lennox.

"Your wife seems but poorly to-day, Aaron," resumed Miss Winter, purposely quitting the other subject.

"She's a bigger ninny than ever," retorted Aaron, in an explosive tone. "I beg pardon ma'am; but the old woman be enough to wear one's patience out."

Dorothy Stone seemed to live in a chronic state of fear. What was it that she was afraid of, her husband would angrily ask her--and the most he could make of her trembling answers was, that she was afraid of the "ghosts." Heron Dyke had become a fearsome place, she would say: any night she might meet Katherine Keen in the passages; or, maybe, the dead Squire. Aaron, quite beside himself with wrath at all this, threatened to shake her: but the threat made no visible impression. Miss Winter would reason with her now and again; but the old woman's life had become a trouble to herself.

What little pleasure (a sadly negative one) she ever found in it, was when she recalled all her grandson's perfections, and her past love for him. To this she found sympathising listeners in the maids.

"Where was there another like him?" she would say, from the easy-chair before the fire in her own sitting-room, a huge black bow on her muslin cap. "So bold, and handsome, and high-spirited--he was fit to match with any gentleman in the land."

"And so he was, ma'am," would make answer to her Phemie or Eliza.

"When was that vision of the hearse and headless horses ever known to show its warning for the likes of you and me?" she would continue; "but it appeared for *him!*"

For it was generally believed that not often was that dire portent visible to mortal eye except when the scion of some great family was about to be summoned hence; thus, as Dorothy looked upon it, the vision must be regarded as a species of honour. It was for Macbeth alone that the witches worked their spells and brewed their potions; their business lay not with the rabble rout that called him captain.

But there came an hour when, pondering upon these matters, it occurred to Edward Conroy, a shrewd reasoner, that more might be in this nervous terror of Dorothy's than she allowed to meet the eye. *What* was it that she was afraid of? He asked himself the question. Sitting by the blazing fire in her own parlour, or in the kitchen bright with sunlight, people around her within beck and call, it could not be that she feared to see a ghost there--that poor Katherine Keen in the spirit would walk in to confront her. Yet, that Dorothy would, and did, sit there often in the day-time in unmistakable terror could not be disputed.

"How much does Dorothy know about the circumstances of your uncle's death?" Mr. Conroy took an opportunity of inquiring of Ella.

"Indeed, I cannot tell," replied Ella. "I have not liked to question her. I dare say she knows no more than we know."

"Um--that's as it may be. She was *here* during all the time."

"Oh yes, she was here."

"Rather a queer notion that of hers, which I hear she has taken up," continued Conroy after a long pause; "that she may meet the Squire's ghost if she goes near his old rooms at night."

"Dorothy was always so silly in that way. You have some motive, Edward, in saying this."

"Yes, I have been watching Dorothy--waylaying her when she steals out to that little patch of herbs which she calls her own garden, and turning in at other times to her sitting-room, ostensibly to hold with her a bit of chat--and she gives me the impression of a woman who has something on her mind; something that will not allow her to rest.

"She has her superstitious fancies."

"I don't mean her fancies. It is a more tangible fear--unless I am mistaken."

"A few days ago I found her crying and trembling," said Miss Winter. "She told me she had dozed off in her chair over her work, and had had a dream which frightened her.

"Did she tell you what the dream was about?"

"No. Except that she thought she saw my uncle in it."

"Ah! It strikes me he is on her mind too much. I wish, Ella, you would put a few questions to her about the Squire, and let me be present."

"Not questions to alarm her, I suppose?"

"My dear, if she knows of nothing wrong in connection with that time, how could they alarm her?"

"True. I will ask her to-morrow morning. She shall come in to take my orders instead of my going to her."

The next morning, Dorothy, full of her cares for dinner, for she was still the housekeeper, and bustling enough in the early part of the day, was summoned to Miss Winter's presence. Mr. Conroy had come to the Hall betimes that day, and sat at the back of the room reading a newspaper.

Ella quietly gave her orders; and Dorothy received them intelligently as usual. In her own department as housekeeper, the woman was capable yet.

"Is that all, Miss Ella?" she asked.

"All for the present. I think of having a few friends to dinner soon; Mr. Philip Cleeve and his wife, and the Vicar; and Lady Cleeve, if she is able to come. Just half-a-dozen or so, besides ourselves--but I will talk to you of that to-morrow."

"Yes, ma'am," assented Dorothy, about to move away.

"Wait a moment," said her mistress. "I wish to ask you a question or two, Dorothy, about that Mrs. Dexter: the woman who nursed my uncle, as I hear, during his last illness. I wish to see Mrs. Dexter. Can you tell me where to find her?"

Dorothy's hands began to tremble as though she had been suddenly smitten with ague. She threw a look at her mistress so frightened and imploring, that the latter almost regretted she had spoken, and then she glanced beyond her at Mr. Conroy: but he seemed to see nothing but his newspaper.

"Do you know where I could find Mrs. Dexter?" repeated Miss Winter.

"I don't know anything about Mrs. Dexter, ma'am," Dorothy whispered forth in a twittering voice. "Nor do I ever wish to know."

"You did not like her, then, Dorothy?"

"I did not like her, ma'am."

Miss Winter rose. "Sit down, Dorothy," she said kindly; "you need not be put out. There, sit in that chair. And now tell me why you did not like Mrs. Dexter."

The trembling woman wiped her lips. "I can't tell why, ma'am. I didn't, and that's all I know. When she first come here with Dr. Jago, I was finely put out; hurt, if one may put it so. My nursing had been good enough for my master up to then, and I thought it might have been good enough still. I told the Doctor my mind."

"Dorothy," continued Miss Winter, after a pause of thought, "I have never questioned you about my uncle's death. The subject was a painful one, and I was more deeply grieved than I can express that I was not allowed to be here at the time. Did you see him up to the day of his death?"

"No," gasped Dorothy.

"When did you see him last? How long before he died?"

Again that same imploring look: but no answer.

"You must tell me, Dorothy."

"Not for weeks and weeks, ma'am," spoke the woman then, but with evident reluctance.

"That was strange, was it not? considering that you were always so great a favourite with Uncle Gilbert."

Dorothy lifted the corner of her clean white linen apron, and wiped her face with trembling fingers. She seemed to gather a little courage. "When he had that Mrs. Dexter, ma'am, he didn't want me, I take it. She was the nurse, and she didn't let anybody go near the master."

"She kept him shut up behind the green baize doors, and would not let him be seen by anyone: that is what you mean?"

"That was just it, ma'am," assented Dorothy, more eagerly.

"But they let you see him after he was dead--you who had been his faithful servant for so many years? Surely they let you look for the last time on that dear face so soon to be hidden for ever?"

"Not even then did they let me see him," she cried. "No, ma'am, not even then. It was cruel--cruel."

"Cruel indeed. I did not think Aaron could have been so unkind to you. He had one of the keys of the green doors, and could have let you through at any time."

Dorothy sighed, and let fall her apron. All this was beginning to frighten her. Miss Winter advanced and stood in front of her.

"There was nothing going on behind those green baize doors, was there, Dorothy?" she asked in expressive tones, her eyes gazing straight into the woman's; "nothing that they wanted to keep from you and from everyone?"

Dorothy flung up her arms with a sudden gesture of dismay.

"Oh, mistress, ask me no more for heaven's sake!" she cried. "I know nothing; I have nothing to tell."

"*Nothing?*" repeated Miss Winter.

"No, ma'am, nothing."

And the poor shaking woman looked so distressed as she crept to the door, that Miss Winter let her escape.

"Ella," cried her lover quietly, rising from behind his newspaper, "it is from that woman we must get the clue. She knows more than she dares to tell. I am right; it is this trouble that is preying upon her mind."

"Certainly her manner is suggestive," assented Ella. "But look at her distress: how shall we get anything more from her?"

"That is just the point we have to consider," said Conroy.

"Of one thing I am persuaded--that she would never tell me what is not true."

"Under ordinary circumstances, no; I believe that. But she may be forced into it by Aaron and the rest of the conspirators."

"Oh, Edward! Conspirators! Poor old Aaron!"

"Well, my dear, time will show. If that old man has not a weighty secret on his back, tell me that my name is not Conroy."

For a few days, after this, things went on at the Hall in their usual state of quiet monotony: perhaps we might say *dis*-quiet, could the minds of some of its inmates have been read. Old Dorothy went about her duties in a dazed manner: but nothing more was said to her.

Gradually, finding herself let alone, the scare, which seemed to have taken up its abode permanently on her face, began to leave it.

"The young mistress must see that I can tell nothing," she told herself, "and she won't frighten me again by asking me to. Why should innocent folks suffer for the guilty? If that Dexter woman and that horrid Jago had but never come anigh this miserable house!"

Late one afternoon, when the sun had set and the dusk of the January evening was drawing on, there was heard a soft knock at the outer door, which opened from the kitchen corridor into the shrubbery at the back of the Hall.

Dorothy was in her own room, adjoining the kitchen, the door between them standing partly open. She had put down the grey stocking of her husband, which she had been mending, and sat in the firelight, doing nothing, save idly watching Phemie, who was preparing her tea in the kitchen, and wondering whether Aaron would be very late. For Aaron and the coachman had driven off to Nullington in the dog-cart, to despatch some matter of business for Miss Winter.

"Wasn't that a knock at the shrubbery-door, Phemie?" asked Dorothy, raising her voice.

"Well, I thought I heard something," replied Phemie, the only servant at the moment in the kitchen. "I'll see directly, ma'am. It's only Jem."

Before Phemie could finish buttering the muffin she had been toasting, the gentle knock was heard at the door a second time. Phemie ran along the short passage and opened it. Expecting to see only the gardener's boy, she started back in some alarm at sight of the strange figure confronting her. Standing between the two lights, one ruddy and homelike that streamed out of the kitchen doorway, the other pallid and ghastly that was dying slowly in the western sky, Phemie saw a tall and fierce-looking woman, tawny-skinned, and with bright black eyes. A scarlet kerchief was bound round the tangle of her black hair; a faded scarlet shawl was draped round her figure and knotted behind. Thick hoops of gold were in her ears; rings glittered on her yellow fingers. A gipsy fortune-teller without any doubt, as Phemie, after the first moment of surprise, at once felt assured. She had seen women attired somewhat like her in the country lanes round about. In her astonishment she did not speak. But the stranger did.

"Don't be afeard, honey. I am only an honest gipsy woman who has lost her way. I want to get to Nullington: being uncertain o' the road, I thought I'd make bold to turn aside here and ask it."

"The road's as straight as you can go," answered Phemie.

"Ah, but it's you that have a pair of wicked bright brown eyes, my lass," whispered the gipsy; "it's you that will make some fine young man's heart ache. Cross the poor gipsy's hand with a bit o' silver, and she'll tell you your fortune true and fair."

Phemie would have liked her fortune told very well indeed: but she glanced back in the direction of Mrs. Stone's parlour beyond the kitchen.

"I daren't do it," she whispered, and tried to shut the door.

By this time two or three of the other girls had come up, and were gathering round. There ensued some laughing and giggling.

"I want to tell your fortunes," said the gipsy, touching one and another in a persuasive, friendly manner. "I heard there was some pretty young women at this place, and I came to it o' purpose. Take me into your bright kitchen there."

"The old missis, she do be in the way," whispered the buxom kitchen-maid, who was from Sussex.

"Sure and the missus wouldn't want to deprive you of hearing o' the future--and the sort o' looks o' the man that's waiting for ye, my lass," returned the gipsy, walking boldly of her own accord into the kitchen. The giggling servants followed her, and one of them dexterously drew to the door of Mrs. Stone's parlour. Phemie hurried in with the tea-tray, which she arranged on the round table; and in going out shut the door.

Bright sixpences were brought forth, hands were crossed with the silver, and the credulous girls listened to "their fortunes." Presently Dorothy Stone, sipping her tea and eating her muffin in quietness, became aware of some unusual sounds, as of murmurings, in the kitchen, interspersed with smothered bursts of laughter.

"What can it be?" thought Dorothy. "They be always up to some nonsense when Aaron's away."

Opening the door, she looked out upon the scene; the wild, formidable gipsy woman seated in her scarlet trappings; and half-a-dozen of the girls standing round her. Dorothy, very much startled at the moment, shrieked out, and the girls looked round.

"What be you all at there?" she called out in a tremor. "Who is that? Sally, this kitchen is not your place; what do you do in it?"

The Sussex girl, who may have been addressed because she was the tallest and biggest, turned her laughing face to her mistress and went into the parlour. Dorothy, not feeling herself very competent to cope with this, was sitting down again.

"Oh, missus, do ye not be angry now," said the girl in her good-humoured way. "We be only having our fortins told; she'll be gone directly. She do be and say as my man'll be a soldier, and I'll have to ride on the baggige-waggin."

Dorothy took heart and courage--what would Miss Winter say if she knew that she had allowed this? "I order you to be gone," she said, her quavering voice marring the implied authority in no small degree. "Go out of the house at once; how dared you to come into it?"

"Who is that?" cried the gipsy.

"Hush! It be Mrs. Stone, the housekeeper," whispered Phemie. "You had better go."

The gipsy woman rose, showing her large white teeth, and strode to the door of the inner room. "Let the poor gipsy tell your fortune, good mistress," she said, with smiling lips and a curtsey.

For once Dorothy was roused to anger. "Go away, you bold woman!" she cried shrilly. "Don't attempt to tell your lies to me. You have told enough to those silly girls."

The gipsy's face darkened; she strode a pace or two into the room. "I have been telling lies, have I? Well, then, let me tell the truth to you:" and, bending her tall form, she whispered a few words rapidly in the old woman's ear.

Dorothy's face turned ashy white as she heard them. She sank back in her chair with a low cry.

"Is that the truth, or is it not?" asked the gipsy.

But Dorothy could not answer. She could only stare tremblingly and helplessly at the fortune-teller.

The gipsy turned to the wondering maids. "Shut that door and leave us together," she said in an imperious tone. "This good mistress here and I have something to say to each other."

The door was closed immediately, and the two women were left alone. The servants waited long enough to grow uncomfortable. What could that strange gipsy woman be doing with the old missis?

"We had better go in and see that all's right," at length spoke Phemie, who had perhaps a shade more thought than the rest, "She may have frighted her into a fit."

At that moment the parlour door was opened, and the gipsy came out. Shutting the door behind her, she strode through the kitchen without a word to the frightened group standing there, let herself out of the house, and departed by the shrubbery, as she had come.

The servants gazed into each other's faces in silence. Then, as with one accord, they opened the parlour door, and peeped in.

Dorothy Stone had her head bent on the table beside the tea-tray, and was sobbing tears, dreadful to hear, of fright, distress, and pain.

CHAPTER X.

THE TRUTH AT LAST

It was a lovely January morning sunny but cold, as the ladies sat around the breakfast-table at Heron Dyke. Miss Winter scarcely spoke a word during the meal, and scarcely touched a mouthful; she seemed buried in thought.

"What is the matter with you, Ella?" asked Mrs. Carlyon, noticing this. "Surely you are not going to be ill!"

"I was never better in all my life, Aunt Gertrude, than I am this morning," answered Ella, with her sweet, serious smile. "Only I do not seem to be in the humour for talking."

"Nor for eating either, apparently," said Mrs. Carlyon with a shake of her cap-strings. "I don't like the symptoms; and if you have not recovered your appetite at luncheon I shall think it time to send for Dr. Spreckley." At which Ella laughed.

By-and-by, Ella put on her hat and shawl and went out, strolling across the garden towards the way in which she might expect the approach of her lover. He was already in sight. Drawing her hand within his arm when they met, he and she paced about for the best part of an hour, talking eagerly. It was the day subsequent to the gipsy's visit to the kitchen, when she had told the fortunes of the maids and--perhaps--of Dorothy Stone, and this conversation ran on that event. The reader will very probably have divined that the gipsy's visit had been a ruse; a thing planned by Conroy, to get some information out of Dorothy.

Going indoors, Ella and Mr. Conroy proceeded to the old Squire's sitting-room, which had not been used since his death. A fire, ordered in it this morning, burnt brightly on the hearth. Ella paused for a moment on the threshold. There was her uncle's big leathern high-backed chair, with the screen behind it, as in the days that were gone. There was the little old-fashioned table with the twisted legs that used to stand at his elbow. It needed but a slight stretch of imagination to fancy that presently the Squire's heavy footstep would be heard, that he would come in with his curt "good-morrow," and begin at once to poke the fire, which was a thing that he believed no one could do as well as himself. Ella's eyes filled with tears.

"Courage, my dear," whispered Conroy. "Think of the present just now, not of the past."

She brushed away her tears and nodded, as she rang the bell. It was answered by one of the maids, Phemie; who was desired to inform Aaron Stone that his mistress waited for him in the Squire's old room.

Aaron received the message with an incredulous stare.

"You must be dreaming," he said wrathfully. "The missus in that cold room--and wanting to see me in it! Be off with your tales."

"Is it cold!" retorted Phemie. "There's a wood fire blazing in it up to the top of the chimney. And the mistress is there, sir, with Mr. Conroy, and she is waiting for you."

Aaron obeyed slowly, fuming a little. He did not like being sent for by Miss Winter and talked to before Mr. Conroy. With all his heart he wished Mr. Conroy well away from Heron Dyke; he was the only man whom Aaron feared. His look of cold, dark, grave scrutiny always disconcerted the old man. What he and Dorothy should do when Mr. Conroy married the mistress and became master of Heron Dyke, which would undoubtedly be the case before long, was a thought that had troubled him a good deal of late.

Aaron paused when he opened the door, and shivered as he looked in. What could he be wanted for in that room, of all others? Had anything been found out?

"Come in, Aaron," said Miss Winter. "Shut the door, and sit down."

She was leaning back in one of the smaller chairs. Mr. Conroy stood against the old-fashioned mantelpiece. The old man took a chair near the door with a sinking heart.

"Some considerable time ago, Aaron," began his mistress in a grave but not unkindly voice, "I put certain questions to you bearing reference to my uncle's illness and death. I had been led to suppose that some mystery attached to that time, and that, whatever it was, it had been kept, and was intended to be kept, from me. You denied it; you told me I was mistaken."

"No, no, Miss Ella, I kept nothing back from you; I didn't indeed," answered the old man, in a trembling, beseeching voice, his agitation pitiable to see.

"But I now know that you did, Aaron. I know that while my uncle was said to have died in the middle of May, he really died weeks and weeks before that date! Will you tell me why you induced me to believe that it was my uncle whom John Tilney and the choristers from Nullington saw on the evening of his birthday, and whom Mr. Plackett, the lawyer from London, saw a day or two later, and whom Mr. Daventry's partner saw--when you knew quite well that it was you yourself, dressed up so as to personate your master, whom each and all of them beheld?"

Aaron's teeth began to chatter.

"The truth is known to me at last," continued Ella. "Do not make any further attempts to deceive me; they will be useless."

"Quite useless," struck in Conroy, a sternness in his tone that Miss Winter's had lacked. "We know all."

What little tinge of colour had been in Aaron's rugged face fled from it; he looked like a man suddenly stricken with some mortal sickness. He turned his affrighted eyes from his mistress to Conroy, and from Conroy to her again.

"Better make a clean breast of it," said Conroy, quietly.

"I will," at length spoke Aaron, in a husky whisper, probably seeing that no other course remained to him. "The Squire did die afore May; long afore his birthday too, the twenty-fourth of April."

"It was a dreadful fraud!" gasped Ella.

"Ay, 'twas a fraud," assented Aaron. "It was not me, though, that set it agate; I only helped to carry it out."

"Who did set it agate?" asked Conroy.

"Hubert: my grandson Hubert. Him and the Squire between them."

"The Squire!" cried Ella, reproachfully. "Aaron!"

"It's true, ma'am. He couldn't rest for fear of dying before his birthday; old Spreckley let him know that he'd not live to see it, except by a miracle, and it a'most killed him. Hubert thought of something. He had been reading just then in one of his French books of a gentleman in France who died and was kept alive for months afterwards--leastways was said to be kept alive, to deceive the world. He told the Squire of this, and the Squire caught at it eagerly; and they spoke to Jago, and he helped to carry it out."

"And you helped too," said Conroy.

"I did it for the best--for the best," sighed Aaron, the tears starting to his eyes as he slightly lifted his wrinkled hands. "Moreover, the Squire ordered me: and when did I ever disobey him? 'Twas in this very room, Miss Ella"-- looking across at her--"that he first spoke to me. I had come in to get him ready for bed, and he told me about it. At the first blush I felt frightened to death; I said to him, 'Master, it can't be done.' 'It can be done, and shall be done; how dare you dissent!' he answered me angrily, and I didn't dare to say more."

What could Ella answer?

"'Twas all for you, Miss Ella; all for you," shivered the faithful old servant--for faithful he was, despite this wrong-doing. "How could you have inherited Heron Dyke had the master not lived over his birthday? 'Twould have gone right away to the other people. A nice thing for that other Denison to have come in to the old place! Swindlers and spies, all the lot of 'em! If----"

"Be silent!" sternly struck in Conroy. "How dare you presume so to speak of your master's kinsman?"

Aaron looked up with a gasp.

"Mr. Denison of Nunham Priors is every whit as honourable as the late Mr. Denison of Heron Dyke. Take care how you speak of him in future. And remember that he is Mr. Denison of Heron Dyke now--and would have been so ever since last April but for your plotting."

Never had Conroy been so moved--so stern.

Ella, though assenting in her heart to every word, looked at him in surprise. Aaron felt checked and mortified; he thought this was pretty assumption for a man who was but a newspaper reporter, and would have liked to say so.

"Mistress," he stammered in a husky voice, "how did you come to know about the Squire?"

"That I must decline to tell you," spoke Miss Winter. "It is enough that I do know it. Had you but told me the truth when I first questioned you, what annoyance it would have saved both myself and you!"

But the aged retainer could only reiterate, "I did it for the best."

Mr. Conroy spoke.

"I want you to tell me, Aaron, the real date of the Squire's death."

Aaron threw a quick, sour, suspicious look at his interlocutor.

"Am I to answer that question, Miss Ella? he asked, in an aggrieved tone.

"Certainly."

"Well, then, if you must know, sir, he died on the 19th of February," was the answer, grudgingly given.

"The 19th of February. What did you do then?"

"Why, what should we do but put the body into a coffin that had been ordered from London two months before by the Squire's own directions. Hubert ordered it, and it was sent down in a packing-case, and the servants were told that it was a new sort of invalid-chair for the master."

"Oh. And this coffin, nailed down, I suppose, was kept in the room?"

"In the lumber-room off the bed-room; nobody had ever thought o' going in there. We kept the room locked mostly after that."

"Just one moment," interposed Ella. "Was the account you gave me of my uncle's death--what happened the evening it took place--a true one?"

"Every word," answered the old man. "Save that it was in February 'stead o' May, ma'am."

"Whose idea was it that you should personate your master after his death?" resumed Conroy.

Aaron did not answer at once. His eyes had taken a dull far-away expression, as though he were lost in the past.

"Such a lot o' things had to be done that wasn't at first thought of," he presently said. "Nobody can foresee what ins and outs a matter will take when it be first planned. Hubert saw that it might not be enough to say the Squire lived over his birthday; people might clamour to see him and convince theirselves of it; and Jago, he saw it also."

"Yes. Go on."

"They thought there was nothing for it but that I must be dressed up to personate him. I fought against it; I did indeed, Miss Ella," lifting his eyes to his mistress, "but 'twas o' no manner o' use my holding out; for, as they pointed out to me, all might have been discovered unless I gave in."

"So they dressed you up!" cried Conroy.

"Hubert did it--the whole scheme was carried out by Hubert. Oh, but he was a clever lad; an amazing clever lad! Jago was deep and cunning, but he had not the talent of Hubert. Who but he got me a wig to imitate the Squire's long white hair, and a velvet skull-cap? I had to put them and the dressing-gown on every day and be drilled for an hour, till I used sometimes to half fancy that I had been transmogrified into the Squire himself. It took in Daventry's partner, and them lawyer rascals from London, finely!--and the band from Nullington and John Tilney and his wife! I had on the cat's-eye ring that the Squire had worn for thirty years."

"Dr. Jago was in the secret from the first.

"Of course he was, sir. He was just the man for a job of that sort, and it couldn't have been done without a doctor."

Mr. Conroy had been jotting down a few notes in his pocket-book.

"I think that is all for the present," he said to Aaron. "If any other questions should occur to me, I can ask them later."

Aaron rose stiffly from his chair. To his ears there seemed an assumption of authority, of power in Conroy, excessively distasteful to him. But the cloud vanished from his countenance and his rugged features softened as his eyes rested on his mistress. No anger, no haughty condemnation sat on that fair young face; only a sort of sweet, patient sadness.

"Miss Ella, you know everything now," he whispered, moving a step or two nearer to her. "But what of that? The world's none the wiser and never need be. The secret's as safe now as ever it was."

"Yes, Aaron, I know everything," answered Ella, a little wearily. "I know that I am no longer the mistress of Heron Dyke. I know that the dear old home no longer belongs to me but to another! But I also know that he will be a worthy inheritor."

Aaron gasped--as if demented.

"But, Miss Ella, you have only to hold your tongue and nobody will ever be a bit the wiser. The Squire bound us all not to tell you, but now that you've found it out for yourself, there's no harm done. You surely would not tell-- no, no! not that--not that!"

"I have no alternative, Aaron. I would do that which is right. This home is not mine: it must be given up to him to whom it rightly belongs."

"Oh, ma'am!--Miss Ella! My master would turn in his grave if he could hear your words. Give up the old place? No--no! And not a soul who knows the secret but ourselves and Jago--and the nurse: and their mouths are sealed!"

"If my uncle, out of that larger knowledge which I doubt not is now his, were permitted to counsel me, do you not think he would urge me to do that which is just and honourable?" said Ella, condescending to reason with him, in pity for his evident wretchedness. "Your master sees now with other eyes than those he saw with when on earth; he would not ask me to keep what is not, and never has been, mine; that which he would have me do, could he speak to me, is the thing I must do, and no other."

Aaron listened, but he was not convinced.

"To think of the estate going to them that the master hated so! Sneaks and spies----"

"Not another word!" severely spoke Miss Winter. "You forget yourself, Aaron."

The old man bowed his head and let his arms fall by his side with a gesture of despair. Turning, he hobbled slowly from the room.

"Poor, faithful old soul!" cried Ella, as she gazed after him. "Wrongly though he has acted, it was done in loyalty to my uncle and me. And so, Edward," she added, bravely smiling through her tears, "you see that you will not have a well-dowered bride."

"So much the better, sweet one," answered Conroy, stealing his arm round her. "You will then owe something to me, instead of my owing so much to you. Nobody can now call me a fortune-hunter."

"They have not called you one."

"Have they not! Ask that old man, now gone out, what he thinks of me in his private thoughts. Ask your Aunt Gertrude; ask Mrs. Toynbee--ask the world."

"I am sure you have never been *that*."

"I don't think I have. But, Ella, it will be a sore parting--this of yours from Heron Dyke."

"I try not to think of it yet. When the day shall come I shall try to bear it as I best may."

"Who knows but that old gentleman at Nunham Priors will give it up to you to live in?" suggested Conroy. "Has he not said something of the kind to you?"

"And do you think I would impose upon his generosity by staying? No, no. This is the place of his ancestors, and it must be his--his entirely; and his son's after him. You forget he has a son, Edward."

"One Master Frank, I believe. A graceless young fellow, by all accounts."

"That may be; but he is still a Denison, and the heir after his father. Besides--you have indeed been speaking without thought, Edward!--how could poor people, such as we shall be, speaking comparatively, live at a grand old place like this? It requires a grand income to keep it up."

"Dear me! So it does."

"You had better give me up, perhaps, Edward, now things have turned out for the worse," she suggested, her voice slightly trembling. "I shall only be a clog upon your ambition, and keep you down."

"Do you think so?" he rejoined gravely. "You will be afraid to venture on marriage with a man so poor as I? Well, there's little doubt you might marry a rich one. Many a man high in the world's favour might be glad to woo and win you. Young ladies with only a tithe of your good looks make rich marriages every season; why should not you? You have always be enused to the luxuries and refinements of life; it would be a misery to me not to be able to afford you them still. Had we not better part?"

Ella was looking at him with a startled expression in her eyes, as if she were half afraid he might be in earnest, and was taking her at her word. Edward Conroy's pleasant laugh rang out. He drew her to him and kissed her tenderly.

"Why, what a great goose you are to-day!" he said. "As if you did not know that our love was altogether independent of either poverty or riches, and that neither one nor the other of them could affect it in any way. You are mine and I am yours, and no caprices of worldly fortune can come between us. And now let us fling our cares to the wind for a little while, and forget everything except that we do love each other, and that the sun is shining, and that Rover and Caprice are waiting to be saddled. Put on your riding-habit and let us go for a long gallop in the sweet January sunshine. If we are not to have many more rides together, it were wise to enjoy them while we may."

When Aaron Stone quitted the presence of his mistress he was like a man utterly dazed and confounded. It was not merely the shock of finding that the elaborate house of cards which he and others had helped to build had tumbled to pieces so suddenly about his ears that dismayed him: it was the fact of Miss Winter's having succeeded in unravelling a plot which had been so patiently planned and so carefully guarded from discovery, that nonplussed the old retainer. So far as he was aware, the secret of the Squire's death could be known to three people alone: to himself, to Dr. Jago, and to Mrs. Dexter: Hubert was no longer living. Both Jago and Mrs. Dexter had been well paid for their share in the affair, and neither of them would be likely to speak of what would render themselves liable to a criminal prosecution. From what unknown source, then, could Miss Winter have obtained her information? Aaron could not answer: and the oftener he asked himself the question, the more puzzled and bewildered he became. As to that bumptious Conroy--one might think the whole place belonged to him to see him and hear his tones!

"There's witchcraft in it, altogether; that's what there is," concluded the dazed old man.

And witchcraft there was in it, but of a kind different from that imagined by Aaron Stone.

Convinced that Dorothy Stone knew more than she dared tell, that the clue to the secret might be got from her by stratagem, though perhaps never by a straightforward examination, Edward Conroy set his wits to work. She was so full of superstitious fancies and beliefs, it seemed to him something might be effected by playing upon them. At first Miss Winter objected, but she grew to see that if the means used were not perfectly legitimate, the end to be obtained certainly was. In fact there seemed to be no other way, and they could not go on living in their present state of uncertainty.

During a recent visit of Conroy to London, he had witnessed a representation of the play of "Guy Mannering," and had been much struck by the powerful way in which the character of Meg Merrilies was portrayed. The actress who played the part was known to the public under the name of Miss Murcott. She was a lady of irreproachable character; and Mr. Conroy had been introduced to her, after the play was over, by one of his newspaper friends. In furtherance of the object he had now in view, he went up to London again, sought an interview with the actress, and enlisted her sympathy. The result was that Miss Murcott went down to Nullington, and took up her abode for a night at Mrs. Keen's, who had been prepared to receive her by Mr. Conroy. In the disguise of a gipsy, and under pretence of telling the maids of Heron Dyke their fortunes, she obtained access to Dorothy Stone, Aaron's absence having been secured by his mistress. Using the information confidentially given her by Conroy, she whispered words into Dorothy's ear that so startled her, as to render her pliable as a lamb.

"Give me your hand," said the sham gipsy: and the dazed and trembling woman held it out without a dissenting word.

Holding the withered palm in her own, the gipsy proceeded to scan it closely, tracing the different lines with her forefinger.

"This indicates a coffin," she said; and Dorothy groaned. "And this--why what *is* this? It seems to point to a hale old man with long white hair, who wears something dark on his head, and is put into the coffin before----"

"Oh, don't, don't!" shrieked Dorothy, trying in vain to withdraw her hand from the gipsy's firm grasp.

"What have we here?" continued the fortune-teller. "A darkened room where people walk with hushed footsteps; green doors that open and shut without noise; a little white-faced man with a black moustache and evil eyes!----And this dark line must be a secret--a secret with a crime in it that might drive you forth from your grave at midnight had you committed it----"

"I didn't commit it," moaned Dorothy. "They never let me know of it."

"No, but you found it out; you hold the secret; this line shows me that. You must disclose it. Tell it at once before it be too late--too late!"

"What shall I do?" sobbed Dorothy: "What shall I do?"

"What I bid you," said the woman, sternly. "Tell me all you know--or there will be no peace for you living or dead."

It needed no more to induce Dorothy to do as she was bidden. With many sighs, and groans, and hesitations, her story came out little by little. It appeared that in those past days the housekeeper's curiosity was aroused, and to a certain extent her anger also, at being kept in ignorance of what was going on behind the green baize doors, and at not being allowed to penetrate beyond them herself. "They treat me as if I was a common pantry-maid," she would say with bitterness. The position also that Mrs. Dexter took up in the household by no means tended to soothe these ruffled feelings. "I've helped to nurse the master for the last twenty years when he has been ill, and now I've got to make room for a strange woman!" she said to Aaron; and all the answer Dorothy got from him was an order to concern herself with her own business. "There's something going on behind those doors that they are afeard to be let known," concluded the shrewd old woman in her mind.

Dorothy determined to go beyond the doors, if she could get a chance of it, and tell her wrongs to the Squire himself; and she watched for an opportunity. It came at last. One afternoon when Aaron had gone to Nullington, he came home all the worse for the pints of strong ale he had taken. Not often did he transgress in this way; and, with the view of hiding it from the household, he went straight to bed, saying the sun had given him a headache, and fell asleep. Dorothy filched the key of the green baize doors from his pocket. Mrs. Dexter, who rarely left the house, had gone this afternoon to the railway-station, to send off some private telegram that she would not trust to anybody else; and Hubert Stone was out riding. In a perfect flutter of excitement, Dorothy took the key to the green baize doors; she ventured to open them both, and went on. Knocking at the door of the Squire's sitting-room, she waited for the answering "Come in." It did not reach her ears. She thought he might be dozing, and opened the door, all in a twitter of eagerness to ask and hear from her master why she was excluded. The room was empty. He is in bed, thought Dorothy, and went to the chamber. That also was empty. She stood bewildered; what could be the meaning of it? Perhaps the Squire had stepped into the lumber-room for something--she opened its door gently, and gave one glance around. That one brief look was quite enough. A low scream broke from her lips; then, hardly knowing what she was about, she closed the door, and fled back by the way she had come. What she saw in the third room was a closed coffin--the very coffin which she saw carried out of the Hall some two months later on the day of Mr. Denison's funeral.

The Squire must be dead; she saw that: but why were they concealing it? Watching and prying about after this, Dorothy, without seeming to see anything, saw enough to convince her that, after the death was really announced to the world, it was no other than her own husband who personated the dead Squire. She stole into the garden the night the musicians were playing, and distinguished Aaron's features in his master's clothes. The day Mr. Charles Plackett was expected from London, Dorothy watched and saw her husband turn back privately, and go stealing into the Squire's rooms, instead of proceeding on his pretended walk to Nullington. All this was confessed to the gipsy woman, who in her turn related it to Miss Winter and Mr. Conroy.

CHAPTER XI.

CONVERGING THREADS

Events now began to follow quickly on the steps of each other.

Philip Cleeve had not yet engaged in any active business. After his return home he had had a slight relapse, and Dr. Spreckley said business must wait. Old Mr. Marjoram, hearing of this in London, for Maria often wrote to him, sent a peremptory mandate for Philip to go back to his house to be nursed. But Philip was getting better now.

Matters were arranged with Mr. Tiplady: and that gentleman had already ordered a new brass plate for his office-door--"Messrs. Tiplady and Cleeve; Architects and Surveyors." The necessary money had been paid by Maria: and the Vicar did not withhold his sanction. Philip would take a fair income for a year or two, then become full partner, and succeed to the whole whenever it should please Mr. Tiplady to retire. It was a very fair prospect, and the Reverend Mr. Kettle saw no cause to grumble at it.

One little clause, known only to Mr. Daventry, who drew it up, to Mr. Tiplady, and to Philip, was inserted in the deed of partnership. It was to the effect that Philip could not come upon the firm for any money whatever beyond his salary; if he contracted debts, Mr. Tiplady was secured from the fear of having to pay them.

"It is only a matter of precaution, Cleeve, inserted as much for your own sake as for mine," Mr. Tiplady said to him in private. "I have not much fear that you will be playing cards for high stakes again, or betting at billiards. Or," added the architect, with a grim smile, "investing your spare cash in silver mines."

"Never again; never again," whispered Philip, tears of emotion filling his eyes, as he clasped the hand of his good friend.

The paying of the money had been a surprise to Mr. Tiplady, knowing, as he did, Philip's penniless state. Without saying a word to her husband, Maria had gone to Mr. Tiplady, and had made over to him the twelve hundred pounds which, long before, he had agreed with Lady Cleeve should be the amount of premium to be paid him in consideration of taking Philip into partnership. How gratifying to Philip it was to know that his mother was never to hear the truth of his folly; that she was to be left in the belief that the money she had made him a loving present of on his birthday, had all gone in the silver mine! In her fond eyes Philip always remained the most peerless of sons. What a weight was lifted off the young man's heart by this generous act of his wife! From that day forward his health improved rapidly; he grew again like the merry, light-hearted Philip Cleeve of old times, his laugh a pleasure to hear. But the lesson taught him was not one to be readily forgotten. And there would be one sweet presence ever by his side to see that his footsteps did not falter, and to cheer him onward whenever the road before him seemed hard and difficult to travel. Philip Cleeve had learnt his life's lesson.

In truth, he had been more lucky than he deserved, and he was to be more so yet. Apart from his past follies, the one item of remembrance that made him wince was the thought that his wife should have sacrificed a great portion of her little fortune to patch up his. Even this bitterness was to be taken from him.

Just at this time his brother, Sir Gunton Cleeve, was despatched to England on some mission by the embassy to which he was attached; and he snatched an opportunity to run down to Homedale for four-and-twenty hours. To him Philip made a clean breast of the past, confessing everything: the card-playing, the billiard-playing, the personal extravagance in the shape of petty ornaments and the like; and the voracious silver mine that had quite finished him.

"Why, what a silly young fellow you must have been!" exclaimed the baronet.

"I know it, Gunton, to my cost. I shall know it all my days."

Sir Gunton had sown a few wild oats during his youth, though he had long ago steadied down, and he was not inclined to be too severe.

"What I don't like, Philip, is this, that your wife should have had to pay the premium to Tiplady. It looks mean--for us. What does the mother say?--and the Vicar?"

"The Vicar has said nothing to me: I don't think he intends to blow me up; he has been very good, I must confess. All he said to Maria was, that the money was her own and he could not interfere. As to the mother, Gunton, she knows nothing of my wicked folly; she thinks the twelve hundred pounds was all swallowed up by the mine. Maria went to Tiplady, and paid over the money without saying a word to anybody."

"Well, look here, Philip. I can't stand this: a Cleeve was never mean yet--at least in our day. I am not rich, as you know, but I can manage this much. I will pay the premium to Tiplady; that is, I will refund the money to Maria: and you had better let it be settled upon her. But I do it in the belief that you will never play at folly again: understand that, young fellow."

The tears had rushed to Philip's eyes.

"Oh, Gunton, you may trust me! How generous you are!"

When Philip had done thanking him, they began to talk of Captain Lennox and the suspicions attaching to him.

"Where is he now?" asked Sir Gunton.

"Nobody knows. He can't be found--by the police, or by anybody else. By the way, you knew him three or four years ago. Gunton."

"*I* knew him!" retorted Sir Gunton. "Knew Lennox!"

"Any way, you have seen him. You met him at Cheltenham, at Major Piper's. Young Conroy, a fellow up at Heron Dyke, told me that much. The Major had a card-party, and you and Lennox were both at it, he said; and the next day the Major's jewels were missing. If you recollect, you spent a few days at Cheltenham about that time."

"Yes, I did; and I recollect the evening. Lennox?--Lennox? Ay, I do remember him now. A fair, slender man of very gentlemanly manners: wore a white rose in his button-hole."

"That's he. One can hardly believe him to be an accomplished swindler."

"If he played these pranks often, helping himself to jewels and purses, and the like, he must have been uncommonly lucky to go on so long without detection," observed Sir Gunton.

"The very remark Conroy made to me."

"Pray, who is Conroy?"

"The luckiest man living," replied Philip, with enthusiasm.

"That's saying a good deal," cried the baronet, lifting his eyebrows.

"Well, upon my word, I think he is, Gunton," returned Philip. "He is nothing but a man connected with newspapers; draws cartoons for them, or something of that. He and Miss Winter met somewhere and fell in love with one another, and she means to marry him and make him the master of Heron Dyke."

"Oh, indeed. What next?"

"I think that's pretty well. You can't say but he is lucky."

"Is the man a sneak?"

"Just the opposite. A highly-educated, open-mannered, masterful kind of man, who can hold his own with his betters, and apparently, not recognise them to be so. To see him and hear him you might think he had been born the master of Heron Dyke at least. Any way, that's what Ella Winter intends him to become."

"She has the Denison blood in her veins, I suppose, and we know the old distich," carelessly remarked Sir Gunton:

"'Whate'er a Denzon choose to do
Need ne'er surprise nor me nor you.'"

The small dinner-party at Heron Dyke, of which Miss Winter spoke to her housekeeper, was held without much delay. Philip, getting strong then, was able to attend it with his mother and Maria. Lady Maria Skeffington, who had been taking a good deal of notice of Maria since her marriage; the Vicar, and Dr. Spreckley completed the party.

Dinner was over, and they were all back in the large drawing-room when the evening post was brought in. It was some hours late; the postman said there had been a break-down on the line. Three or four newspapers came in, and one letter, which was addressed to Miss Winter. It bore the American post-mark; and Ella's curiosity arose, not so much because she knew no one in America, as that she thought the handwriting was Margaret Ducie's.

"Oh, I must open it," she exclaimed, taking it into the next room.

The intervening doors were open, and they watched her read the letter. She came back with it in her hand, looking a little pale.

"It is from Mrs. Ducie," she said in a low tone to her guests: "it is dated from Rhode Island, America. I think you ought to hear it. Perhaps"--turning to Mr. Conroy--"you will read it aloud."

Conroy took the letter from her hand, glanced over it, and began:

"'Mrs. Ducie, late of The Lilacs near Nullington, takes the liberty of addressing a few lines to Miss Winter of Heron Dyke. She does it with great reluctance, as Miss Winter will readily understand; but the charge is laid upon her, and she cannot evade it: the time being now come when certain facts connected with the past must be made known.

"'Mrs. Ducie's brother, known to Miss Winter and to others as Captain Lennox, died two days ago. Enclosed is a declaration which he dictated, word for word, before his death; with a request that it might be forwarded to the proper quarter immediately after that event should have taken place.

"'Mrs. Ducie can make no attempt to palliate anything that happened in the past. As it was, so it must remain. If all were known, which it never can be here on earth, it would sometimes be found that the greatest sinners were first driven into sin by no wish or will of their own. Many, who were destined to fill an honourable career, have been forced by circumstances which they could not control on a contrary path. The dead are sacred; and she, who is obliged to write these painful lines, can never forget that she has lost a brother, who, whatever his faults might be, was dearer to her heart than anyone now left to her.'"

Such was Mrs. Ducie's note. The enclosed paper was also in her handwriting. Mr. Conroy went on to read it.

"'I, Ferdinand Lennox, or the man commonly known by that name, being about to quit this petty planet, and set out on my travels to that unknown country from which there is no return, am desirous, while there is still sufficient strength and clearness of mind left me, to state the facts with regard to a certain event as they really occurred; which facts will probably be found to be somewhat different from what the world believes them to be. I allude to the death of Hubert Stone.

"'The fates had been unpropitious for some time; circumstances were against me; I had lost heavily on the turf and in other speculations, and was nearly at my wit's end for lack of ready money. It was at this time that my sister, quite innocently, told me of the strange discovery of a quantity of old family jewels at Heron Dyke.

"'And, in justice to her, my good and faithful sister, I may here remark that since she came to live with me I have been more cautious, and have striven to keep my little peccadilloes from her knowledge. She may have thought sometimes that my luck at the card-table was something out of the common way, but of the darker passages of my life she knew absolutely nothing.

"'It did not take me long to decide that I must make those jewels mine if it were by any means possible to do so. My circumstances just then were desperate, and a *coup de main* had become absolutely necessary. Burglary was altogether out of my line, but in this case the enterprise seemed to me so peculiarly an easy one that I could not make up my mind to forego it. I knew the position of the room in which the jewels were lying. I knew that it was only a question of opening a window and forcing a shutter, after the family should be safe in bed. There were no dogs to fear, and the servants slept in another wing of the house. Nothing could possibly be more easy. I felt that I could never forgive myself if I allowed such an opportunity to escape me.

"'Up to a certain point, everything happened in accordance with my expectations. The Hall was in darkness; there was no sign of life anywhere. I found the window I was in search of, and a few minutes later I stood inside the room. I opened a slide of my dark lantern and took a survey. There stood the bureau in the corner where I had expected to find it. I had brought a small chisel and one or two other implements with me, and a very little time sufficed to force open the receptacle in which the jewels were stored. What a fine glow filled my heart as I feasted my sight for a few moments on their flashing beauty, and recognised the fact that they were all my own! For some time to come my finances were assured.

"'I was wearing an old shooting-jacket with many pockets, so that I had no difficulty in stowing away my booty. I was putting away the last handful when a noise behind me made me start and look round. There was just enough starlight to enable me to discern the figure of a man standing at the open, window and gazing into the room. Flashing a ray from my lantern across his face, I at once recognised the man as Hubert Stone. A moment later he had vaulted over the low window-sill into the room. 'Surrender, you villain,' he cried, 'or it will be worse for you!' I did not answer, but moved noiselessly in the darkness over the soft carpet to another corner of the room. He was evidently nonplussed, and after standing still for a moment or two I could just make out his figure as he advanced slowly but in a direction opposite to the spot where I was standing. Now was my opportunity. I made a rush for the window, reached it, and was leaping from it; when, as ill-luck would have it, my foot caught against the slightly-raised framework, and I fell face downward on to the gravelled pathway. Hurt and bleeding, I regained my feet, but only to find myself enclosed by the stalwart arms of young Stone. 'Surrender!' he said again. Again I made no answer, hoping he had not recognised me, and a desperate struggle began between us: but he was the younger and the stronger, and presently we were rolling over each other on the ground. It must have been then that I lost the sleeve-link; which loss has led to all the mischief as regards myself. Although I could by no means get away from Stone, he was unable altogether to overpower me. Suddenly, while holding me down with his right hand, with his left he drew from some inner pocket a closed knife, which, with the help of his teeth, he presently contrived to open. 'If you will not surrender,' he said, 'I will mark you so that you can be traced wherever you go.' What he was about to do I know not, but I suddenly struck up my arm, and the knife flew out of his hand. His object was now to regain possession of it, while mine was to keep him from doing so. We were still struggling on the ground; when, I know not how it was, but suddenly my fingers felt the knife as it lay among the gravel. I gripped it instinctively and drew it towards me, and Stone perceived that I had got it. He bent suddenly forward to regain possession of it, but as he did so the point slipped and penetrated deep into his chest. A short sharp cry broke from his lips, he sprang to his feet at a single bound, threw up his hands, staggered a pace or two, groaned, and fell on his face--no doubt dead.

"'Once for all, let me assert most solemnly, and at a time when to tell a lie in the matter could be of no possible benefit to me, that I am utterly guiltless of intentionally causing Hubert Stone's death. His fate was the result of an accident brought on by his own rashness. Had he left the knife in his pocket he would have been alive at the present moment; although how the struggle would have terminated in that case, and what might have happened to me, is another matter.

"'After having confessed to so much, it maybe some relief to the minds of certain people if I reveal one or two other secrets, which in comparison are trifles. Be it known, then, that it was I, Ferdinand Lennox, who appropriated Mrs. Carlyon's jewel-case, and Mr. Booties watch and chain, and the old Doctor's gold box, together with one or two minor articles that I happened to find close to my hands; hands that had acquired remarkable dexterity in the art of conveyancing. And, really, if unthinking people will place such flagrant temptations in the way of poor erring humanity, they are decidedly to blame; for it serves to entice otherwise would-be innocent people into wrong-doing. Had no thoughtless person ever put temptations before me, even my dark plumage might have been far whiter than it is now.

"'And now that my task is over--it has cost me some pain, if only from the sight of my poor sister's tears that drop on her writing as she sits by the bed--I subscribe my name for the last time in this world: FERDINAND LENNOX.'"

It was his own signature, scrawled in a shaky hand.

"Poor Mrs. Ducie!" exclaimed Ella. "I shall write her a nice letter."

"So shall I," added Maria.

"I shall write to her myself," cried the good-hearted Vicar. "If we were all to be abandoned for the sins committed by our friends and relatives, the world would be harder than it is."

"To have had such a brother!--so sweet a woman as that Margaret Ducie seemed to be, poor thing!" lamented Lady Maria Skeffington. "She quite won my heart."

Philip Cleeve's face flushed: Margaret Ducie had nearly won his. He recalled what his feelings towards her had been. But last summer's flowers were not more dead than those feelings were now.

"Mrs. Ducie will never come back to England," he remarked aloud.

"Never," nodded Dr. Spreckley: "we may rest pretty well assured of that. It must have been Lennox to whom you were indebted for the loss of your purse," he added to Mr. Kettle.

"Ay," said the Vicar. "I remember quite well that he stood talking to me for some little time just before the party broke up. The fellow was so pleasant that no one on earth would have taken him for a pickpocket. Dear me! what curious experiences we pick up in life!"

The discovery made of the treacherous plot enacted at Heron Dyke was not to be proclaimed to the world: it reflected discredit on the old Squire as much as on his subordinates, and Miss Winter was anxious to spare his memory. But to one or two people it must necessarily be disclosed, Ella intending to bespeak their secrecy. Mr. Daventry was the first to hear it.

Ella, accompanied by her aunt, proceeded to London, Mr. Daventry travelling by the same train. Conroy had left Nullington the day before, upon business of his own. The object of Ella's visit was to see Mr. Charles Plackett, and inform him that she was now prepared to yield up the property to his client at Nunham Priors. But she meant to ask the favour of Mr. Denison, of being allowed to remain at Heron Dyke herself for a short period longer; until, in fact, she quitted it with Conroy for good: which she felt sure the kind old man would accord.

Ella had told her aunt something, but not all. She gave her to understand that in consequence of some flaw in the title-deeds, Heron Dyke had become the property of the other branch of the family. There is no need to dwell on Mrs. Carlyon's perturbation of spirit when she found that her niece was determined to give up everything of her own free will. Of her own free will: that is how Mrs. Carlyon looked at it. When first the news was broken to her she cried, and implored Ella not to be so romantically foolish, so ridiculously Quixotic. "If there is any flaw in the title-deeds it is their place to find it out, and not yours to show it them," she reiterated. But Ella assured her that she could not help herself; *no other choice was left her*; that in fact the estate had been Mr. Denison's ever since her uncle's death. It a little appeased Mrs. Carlyon; she kissed Ella, and remarked that "what must be, must be."

And, in the gratification of once more getting to her own home, Mrs. Carlyon recovered her spirits. Ella was her guest that night; and the following morning proceeded to keep the appointment already made with Mr. Charles Plackett, Mr. Daventry meeting her there. In a very few words Miss Winter stated her business. Recalling to Mr. Plackett's mind their interview at Heron Dyke and what passed thereat, she went on to state that since that time certain fresh circumstances had come to her knowledge, in consequence of which she had decided to give up the property to Mr. Denison. What the circumstances in question were she declined to say, at least at present, and begged that she might not be pressed to explain. All she wished was that Mr. Denison would quietly accept that which she had of her own free will come to offer him, without inquiring too curiously into the past. In short, Mr. Charles Plackett understood that she wished to have no thought of persecuting this person or indicting that one; there must be a complete condonation of what might have happened in the time gone by. During this, Mr. Daventry sat by and said nothing: he was but there to give, as it were, legality to this avowed resolution of Miss Winter's; in fact, to show the other side that it was not made lightly, or in jest.

"I perceive," nodded Mr. Charles Plackett, gazing at his brother lawyer: "you have obtained information that you consider to be conclusive as to my client's rightful claims, but the particulars of which you do not wish to be inquired into?"

"That is so," replied Miss Winter.

"Is my esteemed friend here, if I may put the question to him, cognisant of these particulars?"

"Yes, I am," spoke up Mr. Daventry. "And I am prepared to testify, if necessary, that Mr. Denison need entertain no scruple whatever as to assuming possession of the estate. Miss Winter resigns it to him from to-day."

Mr. Charles Plackett looked at her earnestly. "It will be a great sacrifice on your part, my dear young lady."

"Yes, it will; I do not deny that," acknowledged Ella, involuntary tears starting to her eyes. "But I have no choice in the matter: none. All I would ask of Mr. Denison is, that he will allow me to remain in the house for a short while longer: a very few weeks at the most."

Mr. Charles Plackett smiled amiably. "That small request will be granted as a matter of course, my dear Miss Winter. *I* remember some words spoken by my client in this very room; not long ago, either. Though it were proved that Heron Dyke did belong to him, he said, he would like that charming young lady to retain it."

Ella smiled faintly, and shook her head. "That cannot be," she answered. "But I do not feel the less indebted to Mr. Denison for the kindness that prompted the thought."

CHAPTER XII.

MORE SURPRISES THAN ONE

Miss Winter remained in London with her aunt three or four days. She had some purchases to make preparatory to her nuptials, and consultations to hold with her dressmaker. Neither did Mrs. Carlyon care to quit her house again without giving a few days to it.

On the morning preceding that on which they were to travel down to Heron Dyke, they were surprised, not knowing he was in London, to see Conroy. He had been somewhere in the country.

"And my visit was a failure," he said to Ella: "the friend whom I went to see was absent from home. I waited a day or two; but as he did not return, I came up here.--Have you been house-hunting?" he carelessly asked.

"House-hunting!" she repeated. "No."

"Seeing that Heron Dyke is to be given up, it will be necessary to fix upon some nest or other, will it not?" he continued.

Ella's eyelashes grew wet in a moment, and she turned away her head. A little while, and the old home that she had known and loved all her life would be hers no longer: how bitter the parting would be, no one but herself could tell.

"And there will be the furniture to select," continued Conroy, in the same light tone; "chairs, and tables, and carpets, and fire-irons, and a thousand other things that we can't do without: but all that I shall leave to you."

"I hope you won't do anything of the kind," said Ella, in some alarm. "I should be the greatest ignoramus in the world at selecting furniture."

"And I should not be one whit better," lamented Conroy. "Mrs. Carlyon, we shall have to fall back upon you. You must purchase for us."

"Time enough for that," returned Mrs. Carlyon, rather crossly. Any reminder of the giving up of Heron Dyke put her out at once. "You intend to travel, you both tell me, for two or three months after your marriage: you can come to me when you return and look out for a house then."

"So be it," said Conroy.

Mrs. Carlyon and Ella returned to Heron Dyke together, Conroy travelling to Nullington with them. Just to make sure that they got down in safety, he observed, laughingly: on the next day, or the next day but one, he should have to go back again.

It was with a heavy heart that Ella entered her many-years home. Not much longer would she be able to call it her own: indeed the feeling of its being hers had already left her. In her heart she began to say farewell to all the sweet familiar places that seemed now almost as if they were a part of herself. No whisper had yet gone abroad of any impending changes at the Hall. Neither had the servants been spoken to. It was best to keep the matter quiet until the last moment drew nearer. So long as she remained at the Hall, Miss Winter did not care to become an object of commiseration, or listen to the condolences of the neighbourhood; after she was gone people might talk as they pleased.

Her thoughts had other things to dwell upon beside the sweet sorrows of farewell. Before her stretched a strange, new, unknown life--a sea whose depths and whose shallows she had not yet fathomed--and sometimes the prospect half affrighted her. But when she thought of Conroy, and how her heart was safely anchored in his love, a trusting courage came back to her. He was the pilot of her life-bark: whatever storms might come, whatever winds might blow, so long as he was at the helm she would not be afraid.

On the morning but one after Miss Winter's return to Heron Dyke, Aaron Stone was crossing the lawn in front of the Hall, when he saw an elderly gentleman within its gates. Pacing to and fro and turning himself about, he seemed to be examining the house from different points of view in a manner that Aaron deemed to be the height of impudence. Aaron had hated strangers all his life, and he made no ado about walking up to this one and demanding by whose authority he was in the private grounds of Heron Dyke.

The old gentleman turned to face him.

"Ah, you are Aaron Stone, I expect: I have heard of you before to-day," said the stranger, as he peered at Aaron through his eyeglass.

"Well, I am Mr. Denison of Nunham Priors. Here is my card. Take it to Miss Winter, and ask her whether she can oblige me with an interview."

Aaron gave a great start at mention of the name, and shrank back a step or two. This little pleasant-faced, inoffensive elderly gentleman the man he had all his life been taught to hate, and whom he had always pictured to himself as more of a demon than a man! He could hardly believe the evidence of his eyes, and stood staring at a respectful distance.

"Take the card, man alive! What are you afraid of?" cried out Mr. Denison.

And there was so much in the impatient, commanding tone, ay, and in the words themselves, that put Aaron in mind of the other Mr. Denison, his late master, now dead and gone, that he took the card at once and hobbled off with it. Mr. Denison watched him with an amused smile. Ella was in her morning-room alone when the old servitor came in with a face white as milk.

"Oh, ma'am! Miss Ella! he has come at last! But don't you see him, ma'am--don't you speak to him. The old Squire will turn in his coffin if you do."

"Who is here?" exclaimed Ella. "Who is it that I am not to see?"

"He is outside on the lawn there, taking his views of the house; but if he once gets inside, there's no knowing what may happen. Keep him out, Miss Ella--keep him out!"

But by this time Ella had the card between her fingers. Flinging down her sewing, she ran out to the lawn with a glowing face of welcome. Aaron's mouth fell. To him the end of the world seemed at hand.

"I am so glad you are come! I am so glad to see you!" cried Ella, with outstretched hands.

Mr. Denison drew the blushing girl toward him and kissed her tenderly.

"You don't know how pleased I am to see you again," he said. "What would I not give if I had a daughter like you!"

"How did you get here? Where did you come from?"

"I came down from London last night, my dear, and was driven to a country inn a mile or two away--I like your old-fashioned country inns, they are pretty sure to be comfortable--and I walked here this morning. I am good for a few miles' walk yet."

"You will come in," said Ella, as she linked her arm in his. "It is your own house now, you know."

"That is a fact with which I shall not be able to familiarise myself for some time to come," replied Mr. Denison. "I have not set foot inside Heron Dyke since I was a lad of nineteen. Dear! dear! what changes in the world, and in me too, since that time!"

They sat down in Ella's pleasant little room overlooking the flower-garden and the park.

"And is this strange news, that Charles Plackett has told me, really true?" asked Mr. Denison.

"Quite true, dear Mr. Denison," said Ella, hiding her quivering lip.

"I was told not to ask any questions, and I won't, although I may have some opinions of my own in the matter, which may or may not be near the truth. However, we will let that pass. I have been anxious to see you ever since I heard the news from Plackett; wishful, too, to see the old roof-tree once again--for I am as much a Denison as my cousin was. But there were two or three interesting sales coming off in London, and I waited for them.----And you are glad to see me, are you!"

"I am indeed. Can you doubt it?"

"Well no, I can't, for your tone and your face tell it me as well as your words. And now, my dear, what I am come to say to-day is this: Heron Dyke must continue to be your home in time to come as it has been in time gone by. However much I may esteem the old place, I should not care to live here: I am too old to change my roof-tree. As regards the revenues, we can come to some arrangement about them after a time. You have behaved so nobly in this matter that I will see you do not suffer, and you may safely leave your interests in my hands. All I wish is that things should go on here as they have gone on hitherto. You shall continue to be mistress of Heron Dyke."

Ella shook her head.

"It cannot be, dear Mr. Denison," she answered through her tears.

"And why can it not be, I should like to know, if I say that it shall be?"

The peremptory tone was her uncle's over again, but with a quaint geniality in it which his had lacked. Ella did not answer at first. Her face was rosy red.

"I am going to be married," she said in a low tone. "So it is not fit that I should continue to be the mistress here: my husband would be the master. And I fear he would not care that his wife should be dependent on anyone's bounty--not even on yours, dear Mr. Denison."

A pained look came into Mr. Denison's face.

"Well, well; I might have had the sense to know that some young fellow would not fail to secure such a treasure. I was foolish enough to dream that you and my boy might perhaps in time meet and learn to like each other, and then--but all that is at an end now. Well, well."

Ella was gazing sadly out of the window. There was silence for a little while.

"I hope the husband you have chosen will take you to as good a home as this, my dear. Is he rich?"

"No. He has four hundred a-year certain, and----"

"Four hundred a-year!" interrupted Mr. Denison, in a tone of contempt. "Why I allow my scapegrace son as much as that. Tut, tut! you can't marry a man who has but four hundred a-year."

"And I have as much, or nearly as much," continued Ella. "Dear Mr. Denison, we shall do very well."

"Very well! After Heron Dyke!" Mr. Denison gave an emphatic sniff. "My dear, I have taken a great liking to you, as much as if you were my daughter, and I don't care to hear of this. I don't approve of it. Four hundred a-year!"

"Is your son come home from abroad?" inquired Ella, to change the conversation, after a pause of silence.

"Oh yes, he has come home, the graceless dog! Came down to eat his Christmas dinner with me at Nunham Priors. Stayed but a day or two, though."

"Is he so very graceless?"

"That's as may be. He thinks himself a model of a son for duty. Reminded me once, when I was blowing him up, that he had never given me a moment's care in his life. Oh, Master Frank's one that won't be sat upon--even by me."

"And has he never given you any care?"

"Care, yes; plenty of it: does he not go roving off by the year together pretty near, leaving me to my china and my things? Is that dutiful? I don't say Frank has vexed me in other ways. He has good parts and principles; he does not play up old Gooseberry, as some young men do. Ah, my dear, if he and you could but have made it out together! You would not have scrupled to stay at Heron Dyke then."

"No, not with him," smiled Ella. "It would have been his own--so to say. We must not think of that."

"No use to think of it, My young gentleman gave me to understand, in an obscure hint or two, that he had been setting up a sweetheart on his own account; hoped to marry her sometime. When I asked who it was, he drew in, and said no more: save that I should know all in good time."

"Then he would not have had me," laughed Ella. "Was it at Christmas he told you this?"

"No, the next time. It was another flying visit that he chose to pay me since then. 'Why don't you see if you can't make up to that young kinswoman of ours at Heron Dyke?' I said to him, and he had the impertinence to laugh in my face. 'Very well, young sir,' said I, 'understand this much: that if you take up with any black foreign woman, let her be a princess if you like, I'll not countenance your marriage.' It was not a black princess, he assured me; so I make no doubt it is some silly native doll."

Ella laughed heartily at the old gentleman's genuine tone of grievance. The next moment she blushed crimson at the sound of a well-known step, and Conroy entered the room.

He stood transfixed with surprise, the door-handle in his hand, as he gazed at the stranger. Mr. Denison rose and gazed back again.

"Sir!" exclaimed Conroy. "What brings you here?"

"I think I may ask what brings *you* here?" retorted the old gentleman, while Ella looked on in wonder. "Have you no welcome for me?"

Conroy advanced and put his hands into Mr. Denison's, his face lighting up with smiles. Ella turned to her lover.

"Do you know this gentleman, Edward?"

"Well, he ought to: he is my own son," interposed Mr. Denison before the other could speak. "A graceless, ne'er-do-well young fellow! always giving me surprises."

Ella Winter stood bewildered. She thought a farce was being played for her benefit.

"This is the--the gentleman I told you of, sir," she said to Mr. Denison. "His name is Conroy."

"Indeed, my dear, it is not. His name is Denison."

"Dear father, it is Conroy; you forget," said the young man with a laugh. "Ella," turning to her, "my name is Francis Edward Conroy Denison, as the church register of my baptism will testify."

"Just you tell me the meaning of this, Master Frank. It seems that you do know your young kinswoman, here."

"Yes, father, and it is to her that I am engaged; she has promised to be my wife."

"Bless my heart!" was all that Mr. Denison could ejaculate. "Conroy? Well, yes, I ought to have remembered that was the name you went by when you chose to go gallivanting about the world as a newspaper correspondent.--My dear, you are looking bewildered--and no wonder."

"I am bewildered," returned Ella.

Conroy turned to address her.

"My father brought me up to no profession," he began. "He thought that as he was a rich man there was no necessity for me to learn to work. With all deference to him I chose to think otherwise. Idleness was distasteful to me. Like Ulysses, I could not bear 'to rest unburnished, not to shine in use.' I wanted to taste the sweet pride of earning my bread by the labour of my own hands. I dropped my family name, and went out into the world; with what result you know."

"You made no such mighty splash after all," grunted Mr. Denison.

"I contrived to be of some use, sir, which was the end I had in view. And I have seen the world, and gained experience. I shall be none the worse for it in the long-run, father."

"And not much the better, I dare say," retorted Mr. Denison. "My dear, can it be true that you have promised to marry this scapegrace?"

"Yes," smiled Ella, with a blush.

"Very good. We'll hold a jubilee. But how was it, pray Mr. Frank, that you kept the secret from me? Is that your idea of duty?"

"Father, I will explain to you; and to you also, at the same time," he added to Ella. "The first time I ever saw this young lady--it was at Mrs. Carlyon's--I fell in love with her. I resolved that she should be my wife, good Providence permitting. Had I been what I then appeared only to be, a correspondent for the newspapers, I might have hesitated to cherish any such hope: knowing myself to be the probable heir of Heron Dyke, certainly of Nunham Priors, I felt the hope was justifiable. In a short while I followed her down here, and got admittance to the Hall, and to Mr. Denison, under the plea of wishing to take sketches of points on the estate: my incipient love for Miss Winter grew into an ardent passion, and I felt assured as to the future. Moreover I saw, or thought I saw, that Heron Dyke would never come to her, but to you; there was that in the Squire's aspect which convinced me he would not live to see his birthday. But now, I must ask you, father, to acknowledge what your course would have been, had I told you this. Should you not have hastened to open negotiations for the alliance with your cousin the Squire?"

"Dare say I might."

"I am sure of it; and that would have ruined all. The Squire would have laid his positive embargo on the marriage, for I was one of the hated Denisons; and he would have extorted a promise from Miss Winter never to see more of me during his life or after it. So I maintained my incognito to her, and said nothing to you. I might have spoken after the Squire's death, that's true enough; but I wanted her to care for myself alone, not for my prospective fortune. I very nearly told you at Christmas, father; but I thought I would wait just a little longer. Last week I went down to Nunham Priors for the purpose, but found you absent. To-morrow I intended to start for Nunham Priors again, expecting you would by that time be at home."

"He should take out a licence for special pleading, he should!" interjected Mr. Denison to Ella. "To hear the neat way he twists and turns things! Where you got your gift o' the gab from, Frank, I don't know. Not from me."

Frank smiled.

"It is true pleading, father. And you need no longer be under the fear that I shall bring home a black wife."

"There's some sense in the 'Dougal creature' yet," muttered the old gentleman, with a flourish of his pocket-handkerchief. "Ah, my dear, what, can I say to him, in what terms can I scold him, when he proffers you to me as his excuse? I can only forgive him, yes, were it a thousand times over!" He drew her to him, and kissed her very tenderly. "You shall be as my daughter--as my own child to me in every way. Heaven has been kinder to me than my deserts--and I am quite sure it has to Frank! And now there will no longer be any question of your quitting the old homestead here."

"But it is yours, sir," answered Ella, through her tears.

"My dear, it is Frank's from this day. I shall never quit my own home of many years. Good gracious! how would all the bric-a-brac be packed and moved? I'll come and see you both here as often as it suits me, and you must come in turn to me."

"And you will stay with me a few days now, to begin with, won't you?" pleaded the grateful girl. "Aunt Gertrude is here, you know."

"Won't say but I will, my dear. I should like to see a bit more of the old family place."

Mrs. Carlyon's surprise when she came into the room and saw the group, and her amazement when she learnt that Edward Conroy the despised was Frank Denison the heir, may well be left to the reader's imagination. Aaron Stone at first refused to believe it: "it was but a trick o' them other Denisons," he muttered, and it did not soften his ill-feeling towards Conroy.

Other troubles were not done with yet. That evening--after dinner--and never had a happier party met under the old roof than was then assembled-- when the ladies went into the drawing-room, Ella was called out of it, by her maid Adèle, to be told that the household was in a commotion. Two of the maids, who had been despatched on some errand to Miss Winter's sitting-room in the north wing, had come rushing down again in a terrible fright, asserting that the ghost of Katherine Keen had appeared to them. As a consequence, the whole of the servants were thoroughly scared. Ella whispered the news into Frank Denison's ear that night before he left for his quarters at the Rose and Crown: but it would take her some time yet ere she could remember to address him by that name. Frank made light of it to Ella, but he resolved to resume his patient watchings; which had been interrupted of late. And his patience was not put to much further trial.

The following evening, Frank--as we must now call him--instead of following his father to the drawing-room, quietly made his way to the north wing. He saw nothing. The next night he saw nothing, heard nothing. On the third night, as he was on the same seat in the darkest corner of the gallery that he was sitting on once before, when he heard those mysterious words spoken, the origin of which he had not yet been able to fathom, he was startled by hearing a low sigh, or by fancying he heard it, no great distance away.

He scarcely dared to breathe. The night was bright with stars and a young moon, and Frank's eyes, accustomed to the semi-twilight, fixed themselves in the direction from which the sound seemed to have come. Next moment he saw a dim figure emerge from the blackness of the corridor beyond and advance slowly into the starlit gallery. As it came nearer, stepping without a sound, he could see that it was robed in black from head to foot, he could see its white face and one white hand that clasped the robe closely round its throat. Frank Denison was no coward; but the figure, gliding noiselessly towards him, looked so eerie and unsubstantial by that dim light, that if his heart sank a little it was hardly to be wondered at. If he, strong and fearless man that he was, felt thus, what must be the effect of such an apparition on the nerves of timid and ignorant girls?

Nearer came the figure, and nearer. It would have passed him without noticing that he was there; but Frank nerved himself, sprang suddenly forward, and flinging out his arms seized the figure firmly round the waist. It felt tangible enough, a form of flesh and blood without doubt: he had half expected that his arms would grasp nothing but thin air. Simultaneously with this, the silence of the north wing was shattered by a piercing scream; and the figure fell into Frank's arms.

That scream did not fail to make itself heard below; two minutes later, half-a-dozen scared faces with as many lights were crowding into the gallery. One of the first on the spot was Miss Winter. She stooped and gently turned the face that was resting on Frank's arm to the light. "Why this is poor Susan!" she exclaimed. "Susan Keen!"

"Susan Keen!" repeated the wondering maids, pressing round.

Mrs. Carlyon was up now. "It can't be Susan Keen: what should Susan Keen do here?" she cried, full of incredulity.

"It is Susan: no mistake about that," said Frank. "The first thing to be done is to try and restore her to consciousness."

The girl was carried to Miss Winter's dressing-room, and placed on the sofa near the fire: the same sofa that Maria Kettle had lain on when she got her fright. Susan soon revived, and they gave her some warm wine. Shutting everybody out except Mrs. Carlyon, Ella soothed and comforted the girl with pleasant words. Gradually the eyes lost their frightened look, and the poor fluttering heart began to beat more equably. Then she was gently questioned;

and, little by little, without much pressing, Susan's story was told by her own lips.

Possessed by the belief that her sister, either alive or dead, was hidden somewhere inside the Hall, poor Susan, as we already know, whenever she could escape her mother's vigilance, took to wandering about the grounds in the dusk of evening, gazing up at the windows of the old house, more especially at her sister's bedroom window, often fancying that she heard Katherine's voice calling her, and trying everywhere to find some traces of the missing girl. After a time the thought seemed to have entered her head that if she could only get inside the Hall and search there, it would be better still. It would appear that on two occasions during Katherine's service there, when Susan had gone up to the Hall hoping to see her sister, Aaron Stone had locked up for the night. Susan had then thrown some pieces of gravel at her sister's window, in order to attract attention; upon which Katherine had come out to her, kissed her, and bidden her to return home. Susan, curious to know by what means her sister had been able to leave the house after it was made safe for the night, had persuaded Katherine to tell her.

Among other rooms on the ground-floor at the back of the Hall, or rather at its side, and the side not frequented, was one that was called the wood-room, in which logs were kept to dry for winter burning. The unglazed window of this room was protected by horizontal iron bars; and one day, by a mere accident, Katherine saw that the lowest bar was loose in its socket; it could be displaced and replaced at will, and there was not the smallest difficulty in stepping through the low aperture to the ground outside. Katherine had thought it no harm to make use of this discovered means of egress on the one or two occasions she had seen her poor simple sister waiting, rather than let the girl remain there, as she might have done, for half the nights When the loss came, poor Susan never spoke of this, lest it might bring blame on Katherine's memory.

But she did not forget it. And when, impelled by uncontrollable longing to discover a clue to her sister's fate and to venture inside the house, she sought for the window, she readily found it. She had but to displace the bar, step in, and be within the Hall. Near the door of the wood-room was a narrow, back staircase, hardly ever used, which led up to the north wing, and so to the bedroom which Katherine had occupied.

Susan Keen might be half-witted, but she was cunning in this search. As she had found a way of getting into the Hall, so she found a way of getting out of her mother's house. After she was supposed to be safe in bed, she would creep downstairs, open one of the lower windows, go out of it, and return in the same way, Mrs. Keen being none the wiser. She made for herself a pair of list shoes which she slipped on over her ordinary walking shoes whenever she ventured, which was but rarely, inside the Hall. Between the two sisters there was a strong family likeness; both had the same long, pale, serious face, the same large, grey eyes, and hair of the same tint--a dark brown with a gleam of gold in it. In the dusk of evening or by the dim light of a candle in a big room, it was quite possible that one sister should be mistaken for the other, even by those to whom both of them were well known. Susan it was whom the two maids, Ann and Martha, had seen looking down upon them from the gallery; she it was who had frightened Mrs. Carlyon and deceived Maria Kettle; it was her voice that Conroy had heard calling for her sister as she wandered through the dark passages of the north wing; it was she who had tried Betsy Tucker's door the night of the storm: and it was no other than she who had rearranged the furniture in Katherine's abandoned chamber, about which there had been so much speculation. The supposed ghost, haunting the north wing, had not been a ghost after all; instead of being Katherine dead, it was Susan living.

"But she will not come to me, though I seek for her everywhere," wailed poor Susan, as she came to the end of her narrative and looked piteously into the compassionate face of Miss Winter. "Oh, ma'am, where can she be? Living or dead, she *must* be inside these walls. I hear her voice calling to me, but I can never find her. Where can she be? where can she be?"

It was a question that Miss Winter could not answer.

CHAPTER XIII.

THE LAST MYSTERY SOLVED

"It's not a bit of use your making any objection, my dear. I've set my mind on it, and I mean to do it. Why should you wait till I'm dead? I may live for a dozen years to come, and the income will be of far more use to you now when you are setting up housekeeping than it would be later."

The speaker was Lady Maria Skeffington, and the person to whom she was laying down the law in this peremptory fashion was her god-daughter, Maria Kettle--or rather Mrs. Cleeve. Maria and Philip had moved into a pretty little house near Homedale; they were furnishing it and beginning life on their own account. Maria had a large apron on, and her gown-sleeves turned up at the wrists; she was making herself as busy as a bee this morning, with her two maid-servants, when interrupted by her godmother.

Lady Maria sat down on the sofa, causing Maria to sit by her side, and began to talk. After a little gossip touching the sayings and doings of the neighbourhood, she went on to tell Maria that she had always intended to bequeath to her two thousand pounds at her death: but that, as Maria was now married, and help would be useful to her and her husband, she had decided to make over that sum to her without delay. It was well and safely invested, and would bring in one hundred pounds yearly, secured to Maria herself.

Overpowered by the unexpected kindness, Maria remonstrated. It was too much, she said: and why should Lady Maria deprive herself of this much yearly income before her death?

"Not another word, child, if you love me. Don't I tell you I have already decided? After that, argument is useless--a mere waste of breath."

Maria knew of old that when once her godmother had made up her mind to any particular course nothing could move her from it. In such a case submission was the only policy. She turned and kissed her. "You are far kinder to me than I deserve, dear Lady Maria! Philip will scarcely know how to thank you sufficiently."

"Philip is not so high-flown as you," rejoined her ladyship, drily. "He knows the value of money; he would never think of refusing such a gift."

Maria said nothing, but she smiled to herself to hear Philip spoken of as one who knew so well the value of money. Though, indeed, his late experiences had perhaps taught it him.

"And now, my dear, I want you to put on your bonnet and accompany me to the Hall," continued Lady Maria. "My barouche is at the door, and I am going to call there. The drive will do you good this bright, brisk morning."

The young wife would rather have been left to the arrangement of her household gods; but she could not refuse her godmother, especially at the moment when she had been so generous to her. So she made herself ready, and they were soon bowling along the road to Heron Dyke. Lady Maria was still full of the marvellous revelation that Edward Conroy was Edward Denison, though some two or three weeks had elapsed since the fact became known abroad.

"I was talking to Dr. Downes about it yesterday, my dear. He agreed with me that it was like one of those romances one gets out of the library. What a good thing it is that the young man is so charming; and indeed I think we might all have seen something in him above an ordinary newspaper reporter."

"It is a romance," agreed Maria, "and a very delightful one. Have you seen Mr. Denison?"

"I saw him when I was at the Hall the other day. A charmingly quaint old man, who put me so much in mind of the late Squire!--And, my dear," added Lady Maria, lowering her voice, lest the servants on the box in front of her should hear, "what do you think Dr. Downes told me--that the ghost which has been supposed to be haunting the north wing has turned out to be crazy Susan Keen."

"It is so," answered Maria.

"The poor half-witted girl has been in the habit of creeping into the Hall at night, to look for her sister, the Doctor tells me. The appearances that were set down to the dead girl, the mysterious noises, and all the rest of it, have been traced to her."

"Susan confessed it voluntarily," remarked Maria. "It is a sad thing--though of course it is well that it should have been discovered."

"Well, Maria, what I should do with the girl is this--put her into an asylum. Dr. Downes agreed with me that many a one has been confined for less cause: though he thinks there will be no further trouble of this sort with her in future."

"Never again in future," said Maria, shaking her head. "Her mother will take right good care of her. She has had a little bed put up for her beside her own, and does not trust her out of her sight."

"Here we are!" cried Lady Maria, as the coachman drove into Heron Dyke. "What a commotion the place seems in! What can be going on, I wonder?"

Mr. Denison found himself so comfortable under the old family roof-tree that he let Nunham Priors take care of itself for a while, and stayed on. Before a week had gone over his head, he was projecting no end of improvements: this must be done, and the other must be done: some for embellishment, some for use; and all, of course, for the convenience and benefit of his son and daughter-in-law, who would inhabit the place. Energetic as ever was the old Squire when once he took a thing into his head, Mr. Denison was not content with projecting: he set about doing. Calling Mr. Tiplady to his counsels, and after him a clever builder of reputation, the alterations were begun forthwith. Heron Dyke was, of course, his own, and he could do what he would.

The new conservatory, recently built by Miss Winter, was all very well, but not large enough; it was to be considerably lengthened and widened.

"I don't like walking down a greenhouse, my dear, where the space allowed for the paths is so narrow one's coat-tails must brush the plants on either side," he remarked to Ella.

The kitchens and some other portions of the domestic offices must be rendered more commodious, in accordance with modern requirements. A new road was to be driven through the shrubbery, and the old, narrow, inconvenient road, rarely used, on the side of the house, blocked up and planted over.

On the morning that was to witness the call at the Hall of Lady Maria Skeffington and Philip's wife, the workmen were busy with this last-mentioned work, when Frank Denison came hastily into the room where his father sat, talking to Ella, Mrs. Carlyon, and Mrs. Toynbee. Frank's countenance wore a startled expression, and he looked grave and pale. Ella's thoughts flew to the men: she feared some accident had happened.

"What is it?" she cried, rising from her seat. "Are any of the men hurt?"

"No, no, the men are all right," he answered. Then, after a pause, he held something out to Ella. "Do you chance to know this?" he asked. "Can you tell to whom it belonged?"

It was a small gold locket, dented in on one side and much discoloured, as if it had lain for some time in a damp place. Ella recognised it with staring eyes, and began to tremble with a fear she did not wait to define.

"This was Katherine Keen's; it was my present to her on her birthday, and she had it on the night she was lost. Oh, Edward, where did you find it?"

"I fear," he replied, "that we have found *her*."

"Found her! Katherine?"

Mrs. Carlyon put Ella back with her hand.

"Sit down, my love," she said. "Frank"--turning to him--"do you say you have found Katherine Keen?"

"I believe so. It can be no other."

"Dead?"

"Oh yes, poor girl."

"But where?"

"In that old well just beyond the wood-room. The men have been uncovering the well this morning, and--and--they have found some one lying in it. She had this locket round her neck."

Ella sat down, white and silent, and hid her face amid the sofa-cushions. Mr. Denison caught up his stick, and hurried out. The news had already got wind. People were running to the spot; and it was just then that Lady Maria's carriage drove in. They had indeed found poor Katherine Keen.

We must trace back to the time of Katherine's disappearance. This old well, situated not far from the door of the wood-room, had supplied the Hall with water for more than a hundred years. But at length, for some unknown cause, the spring had begun to fail, the water in the well gradually becoming lower, until what was left lay so deep down that it was not worth the labour of drawing up. After that, the old well was left to itself for several years, the woodwork above it. decaying and rotting slowly in summer sun and winter rain. It lay, as has been said, on the unfrequented side of the house.

"I'll have this altered," said the Squire one day as he chanced to pass that way, and stood to look at it; and he at once gave orders that the woodwork should be removed and the well filled up.

His wishes were not long in being carried out. The old woodwork disappeared, a quantity of earth and rubbish was collected to be shot into the well, and a large flag-stone, big enough to cover the whole of the orifice, was brought to the spot. The work was in progress one February afternoon, when the snow began to come down thick and fast, which caused the men to cease working until the morning, only a portion of the filling-up rubbish being then shot in.

Except the actual fact of the catastrophe itself, what else happened on that fatal night could only be matter of conjecture. The inference was, that Katherine, on reaching her bedroom and beginning to undress, lifted up a corner of the blind, and, peering out, saw her sister standing below gazing up at the window, a dark figure outlined against a snowy background. The snow by this time had ceased to fall, and a bright moon was struggling through the broken clouds. Katherine must then have hurried downstairs with the intention of seeing her sister and sending her back home. Although the house was being locked up, she would get out easily, and unseen, by the wood-room window, replacing the loose bar as a matter of precaution. This done, she no doubt ran round by this unfrequented way where the well was, and fell headlong into it, the two screams heard, one loud, the other fainter, escaping her in the act of falling. Whether she cried out afterwards, and there was no one to hear, or whether she fell senseless, or whether she was killed at once, must remain matter of supposition. After that, so far as was known, all was silence.

Early next morning came the workmen. More snow had fallen in the night, erasing all footprints of the previous evening, covering the bottom of the well with a white surface. The men made sharp haste to finish their task, knowing and suspecting nothing; and Katherine's fate had remained undiscovered until now.

Aaron's habitual crustiness had something to do with the nondiscovery. Chancing to meet the men as they quitted the work before time that evening, he sourly demanded whether the work was accomplished and the well filled up. Afraid of him, not caring to incur his stinging reprimands, both the men answered that it was quite finished. Therefore Aaron never gave a thought to the well in regard to Katherine's disappearance; and as for the Squire himself, and the rest of the household, they did not so much as know that the work was just then about. While the fact of its being impossible, or assumed to be, that Katherine could by any manner of means have got out of the house, served yet more to divert thoughts from the truth. And the two workmen, deceived by the white surface inside, on which they had both looked down in the morning, never, then, or later, supposed the well could have anything to do with the girl's disappearance.

Thus the last and longest mystery was solved. Such had been poor Katherine's unhappy fate. Susan would never more wander in the park after nightfall, or within the Hall to look for her; she would never hear her sister's voice calling to her again, never fancy that the moonlight playing upon the window of Katherine's room was her apparition standing there.

The wedding was a very quiet one. Without show or parade, Ella Winter became the wife of that erratic gentleman, Francis Edward Conroy Denison, the indisputable heir of Heron Dyke. Old Mr. Denison insisted upon giving the bride away; and a hamper of his choicest china arrived from Nunham Priors to deck the breakfast-table. Lady Maria's nephew, the young Earl of Skeffington, had asked leave to be the best man.

Aaron stood behind his mistress's chair at breakfast; to deny him this privilege would have broken his heart; but it was the last service he would render at the Hall. He and his wife were about to retire to a pretty little cottage near the Leaning Gate: Mr. Denison, at Ella's wish, had given it to them for life, and she had furnished it.

Frank and his bride, now Mrs. Denison, as her uncle had always wished her name to be, started on their way to the Continent. During their absence, which might extend to two or three months, the alterations at Heron Dyke would be completed, and their establishment put upon a proper footing.

What more is there to tell? All are left happy. The years go round, and as yet no sorrow falls. The young Squire, as Frank Denison is now called, is in Parliament, so that he and his wife are much in London during the earlier portion of the year. Mr. Denison travels often from Nunham Priors to stay at Heron Dyke, where his pleasantest days are passed. When Ella's baby came, he was a little grumpy in his comical way at its being a girl, instead of the boy he had expected: though he acknowledges that it is not impossible the boy may put in an appearance later.

Much unity, friendship, and intimacy exist between Ella and her husband and the Cleeves. Philip is so steady as to justify his mother's never-changed fond opinion of him; his talents for business and his application to it surprise even Mr. Tiplady: while his laugh is as genial and his manners are sunny and pleasant as ever. Little Freddy Bootle often runs down to see them, and is ever a welcome guest at the Hall. Mrs. Carlyon comes sometimes, and the baby bears her name, Gertrude.

Even old Aaron is tolerably happy--for he can grumble to his heart's content. He could not cease from doing that. Partly at Dorothy, though she does not mind it, partly at his friends in general. He is a great man of an evening in the sanded parlour of the Leaning Gate, or the Fisherman's Arms. A special chair is placed for him, and he, between the intervals of growling at the world, tells anecdotes of forty years ago to the deferential company smoking around.

Mrs. Keen, active as of yore, is assisted in her duties by Susan. Time has laid its healing hand upon their sorrows. Poor Susan will never be quite bright, and that half-dazed look is sometimes to be seen on her face still; but no sweeter-tempered or more gentle girl is to be met anywhere; and now that the mystery of her sister's fate no longer weighs upon her brain, there is a sort of peacefulness and soft serenity about her which are very attractive. Her greatest treat is to go up to the Hall and see the baby, little Gertrude; and the nurses avow that that youthful tyrant is never so much on her good behaviour as when allowed to rest for a few minutes in Susan's loving arms.

But as soon as ever daylight begins to die in the woods round Heron Dyke, when the long corridors of the old house grow dim and the wide staircases become the homes of shadow and mystery, then does Susan resolutely set her face homeward. She who used to haunt the Hall after nightfall, when trying to find the ill-fated Katherine, will not go near it except in broadest daylight.

END OF VOL. III.

Milton Keynes UK
Ingram Content Group UK Ltd.
UKHW012313040624
443649UK00007B/597

9 789361 470448